GOOSEBUMPS
Also available as ebooks

P9-BYT-475

NIGHT OF THE LIVING DUMMY

DEEP TROUBLE

MONSTER BLOOD

THE HAUNTED MASK

ONE DAY AT HORRORLAND

THE CURSE OF THE MUMMY'S TOMB

BE CAREFUL WHAT YOU WISH FOR

SAY CHEESE AND DIE!

THE HORROR AT CAMP JELLYJAM

HOW I GOT MY SHRUNKEN HEAD

THE WEREWOLF OF FEVER SWAMP

A NIGHT IN TERROR TOWER

WELCOME TO DEAD HOUSE

WELCOME TO CAMP NIGHTMARE

GHOST BEACH

THE SCARECROW WALKS AT MIDNIGHT

YOU CAN'T SCARE ME!

RETURN OF THE MUMMY

REVENGE OF THE LAWN GNOMES

PHANTOM OF THE AUDITORIUM

VAMPIRE BREATH

STAY OUT OF THE BASEMENT

A SHOCKER ON SHOCK STREET

LET'S GET INVISIBLE!

NIGHT OF THE LIVING DUMMY 2

NIGHT OF THE LIVING DUMMY 3

THE ABOMINABLE SNOWMAN OF PASADENA

THE BLOB THAT ATE EVERYONE

THE GHOST NEXT DOOR

THE HAUNTED CAR

ATTACK OF THE GRAVEYARD GHOULS

PLEASE DON'T FEED THE VAMPIRE

ALSO AVAILABLE:

IT CAME FROM OHIO!: MY LIFE AS A WRITER by R.L. Stine

SLAPPY NEW YEAR!

R.L. STINE

SCHOLASTIC INC.
New York Toronto London Auckland
Sydney Mexico City New Delhi Hong Kong

If you purchased this book without a cover, you should be aware that this book is stolen property. It was reported as "unsold and destroyed" to the publisher, and neither the author nor the publisher has received any payment for this "stripped book."

No part of this publication may be reproduced, stored in a retrieval system, or transmitted in any form or by any means, electronic, mechanical, photocopying, recording, or otherwise, without written permission of the publisher. For information regarding permission, write to Scholastic Inc., Attention: Permissions Department, 557 Broadway, New York, NY 10012.

ISBN 978-0-545-16199-2

Goosebumps book series created by Parachute Press, Inc.

Copyright © 2010 by Scholastic Inc.

All rights reserved. Published by Scholastic Inc., *Publishers since 1920*. SCHOLASTIC, GOOSEBUMPS, GOOSEBUMPS HORRORLAND, and associated logos are trademarks and/or registered trademarks of Scholastic Inc.

12 11 10   17 18 19/0

Printed in the U.S.A.   40
First printing, November 2010

MEET JONATHAN CHILLER . . .

He owns Chiller House, the HorrorLand gift shop. Sometimes he doesn't let kids pay for their souvenirs. Chiller tells them, "You can pay me *next time*."

What does he mean by *next time*? What is Chiller's big plan?

Go ahead — the gates are opening. Enter HorrorLand. This time you might be permitted to leave . . . but for how long? Jonathan Chiller is waiting — to make sure you TAKE A LITTLE HORROR HOME WITH YOU!

PART ONE

My name is Ray Gordon and I'm twelve. My brother, Brandon, is nine, but people think that he's older than I am.

That's because Brandon is a big hulk of a kid. He's about half a foot taller than me. He has broad shoulders and a big chest, straight black hair, and a cold stare that makes him look like he's tough.

I'm short and very thin. I have curly blond hair and blue eyes and freckles on my cheeks. I'm the youngest kid in my class, but I'm three years older than Brandon. And everyone we meet thinks I'm the little brother.

Which is funny because Brandon is a total wimp. So *what* if I look like an elf standing next to a giant?

I'm the tough one in the family. He's scared of bugs and snakes and being in the woods and being in the water. And anything else you can think of.

And once I actually saw him jump away from his own shadow. No kidding. He swore he tripped. But I know the truth.

It's a pain having a younger brother who's bigger than me. And it's an even bigger pain having a huge monster brother who is a total coward.

I love scary movies. But my parents say I have to go to G-rated baby movies with Brandon so he won't get scared. I like to watch scary TV shows, too. And play really cool battle games on my Xbox.

But guess what? I'm not allowed while Brandon is around. We don't want to upset the poor guy — do we?

And now . . . even worse . . . he's ruining my first trip to HorrorLand.

He's too scared to do anything. The rides are too scary for him. The games are too noisy and frightening. The Haunted Theater is too *haunted*!

He's even afraid of the Horrors. They're the big, furry, green-and-purple park workers. You know. They are guides, and they run the rides and the game booths and work in the shops.

Brandon is almost as big as they are. But he's terrified of them.

So how much fun am I having with him at HorrorLand? Can you spell *zero*?

It was a cool, gray day. Wisps of fog hung low

4

over the park. A perfect spooky day to be at HorrorLand.

"Brandon, what if we go on the scariest ride here?" I said. "What if —"

"I don't want to," he said. His favorite expression. He sticks out his lower lip and gets all pouty and says, "I don't want to."

"No. Listen to me," I said. He was staring at a Horror behind a food cart. I grabbed his arm and tried to turn him around. But I wasn't strong enough to budge him.

"What if we both go on the scariest ride ever," I started again. "And you *like* it? Wouldn't that be great? Wouldn't you think it was cool to find out that you like scary rides, too?"

"But I don't *want* to," Brandon whined.

I sighed. Mom and Dad let Brandon and me go off on our own this afternoon. And I didn't want to waste it doing baby stuff.

I dragged Brandon up to a tall green Horror wearing bright yellow overalls with yellow suspenders. He wore a button on his cap that read: I'M A SCREAM!

He grinned at me. "Hey, kiddo — know why I wear yellow suspenders?" he asked.

"Why?" I said.

"To keep my pants up!" He roared with laughter and slapped his knees.

"That's a very bad joke," I said.

"No, it isn't," the Horror replied. "It's a SCREAM!" He opened his mouth and screamed at the top of his lungs.

Brandon covered his ears.

The Horror tapped the button on his cap. "Just doing my job," he said. He coughed. "I get *such* a sore throat from this job! What can I do for you?"

"My brother and I want to do something way scary," I said. "What's the scariest ride in HorrorLand?"

The Horror rubbed his furry chin. "Have you tried the Doom Slide?"

"Too scary," Brandon said, doing his pouty face.

"I did it without him," I said. "It was okay. But not great."

"How about the A-Nile-Ator coaster?" the Horror asked. "It's the world's only coaster where you ride in a coffin."

Brandon shivered and shut his eyes. "Not for me," he whispered.

"It was good. But not really scary enough," I said.

The Horror stared at me for a long time. He rubbed one of the curled horns on either side of his cap. "Okay, I get it," he said. "You want something to make you scream like *this*."

Again, he opened his mouth, tossed back his head, and let out a bloodcurdling scream.

6

"Yeah. Like that," I said.

"I get it," he said. "Okay. Come with me, guys. I'll take you to our test area. It's where we try out new things. Not open to the public. You can be the first to try them."

"Awesome!" I cried. My heart started to pound. "Totally awesome!"

The Horror turned and started to walk quickly away from Zombie Plaza. I saw where we were headed — a fenced-in area with a big sign: TESTING AREA. KEEP OUT!

I jogged to stay up with him. I had to keep turning back and waving frantically to Brandon to follow us.

Brandon kept shaking his head. "I — I have a bad feeling about this," he muttered.

Maybe I should have listened to him. . . .

The Horror unlocked a gate and led us to the other side of the fence. We followed him into a huge white bubble. It looked like one of those domed tennis court places.

Our footsteps echoed as we walked inside. I gazed around. The building was as big as a football stadium.

In front of us stretched a long, oval-shaped racetrack, with several lanes marked in yellow paint. Sitting on one end were about a dozen little red racing cars.

A small sign on the wall read: TEST TRACK — THE SHOCKER.

The Horror led us onto the track. "I'm going to let you be the first kids ever to try out these race cars," he said. "They're real cars. You control them."

"Cool!" I cried.

"Wh-why do they call it The Shocker?" Brandon asked.

"You'll see," the Horror replied.

The cars were open — no roofs. I swung a leg over the side of the nearest red car. Then I lowered myself onto the seat and settled behind the steering wheel.

Brandon squeezed into the car next to mine. It was so small, he filled up the entire seat. "Hey — there's only one pedal!" he cried.

"That's the gas," the Horror said. "There is no brake."

"But — but —" Brandon started blinking his eyes rapidly. He does that whenever he starts to panic. Which is all the time.

The Horror patted him on the shoulder. "You'll be fine, kid," he said. "This ride is going to be a *scream!*"

"But I don't *like* to scream!" Brandon cried.

"Just stay in your lane, and you'll be okeydokey," the Horror said. "Don't swerve into another lane. If you do . . ." His voice trailed off.

I lowered my foot onto the gas pedal. The little car let out a roar. Then it started to move forward.

I gripped the wheel with both hands and leaned toward the low windshield. The yellow lanes stretched far in front of me. The car moved slowly at first. I steered carefully, keeping it straight.

"Wow!" I screamed over the roar of the engine. "This is totally awesome!"

9

Out of the corner of my eye, I glimpsed my brother. His car was coming up beside me on the right. He stared straight ahead. He gripped the steering wheel so tightly, his knuckles were *white*!

Into the first turn. My car started to pick up speed. I turned the wheel and followed the curve of the turn.

Behind me, I heard Brandon's tires squeal. I kept my eyes straight ahead. I couldn't look back.

My car roared down the straightaway. The hot air of the closed building rushed against my face.

My heart pounded. I zoomed around the next turn, carefully keeping in my lane. I could hear the roar of Brandon's car close behind me.

This is totally like being a NASCAR driver! I thought. *Way cool!*

"Whoa!" I nearly swerved into Brandon's lane. I gripped the wheel and swung it hard to the left.

I lifted my foot off the gas. But to my surprise, the car didn't slow down. It sped up!

Faster. The track appeared to tilt up and down. The tires beneath the little car bounced hard.

I leaned forward, my eyes locked on the yellow lines in front of me. *Faster.* And the lines became a bouncing, throbbing blur.

Into a hard turn.

"I can't control it!" Did I scream those words or just think them?

The wheel jerked in my hands. The car bumped. Bumped again. And I swerved over the yellow line — into the next lane.

BUZZZZZZZZZZZZ.

A powerful shock rocked my whole body. The sound roared in my ears. My hands shot off the wheel. My muscles tightened and froze. Pain zigzagged up and down my arms and legs.

I shook my head hard, trying to get the buzz of the shock out of my ears.

"OW! That HURT!"

Still gasping for breath, I grabbed the wheel. I spun it hard to get back in my lane.

I saw Brandon's car roar up beside me — too late.

I crashed into him hard. My car spun into the center of the track.

As I spun, I saw his car smash into the rail at the side.

BUZZZZZZZZZZZ.

We both screamed. Powerful shocks rocketed through me. My whole body shook and vibrated.

I gripped the wheel and swung my car back into the right lane.

"This is HORRIBLE!" I heard my brother's scream as my car roared away.

I turned to see if he was okay —

— and my car squealed as it scraped the railing.

BUZZZZZZZZ.

Another powerful shock. And the car screeched to a dead stop.

Silence now. Except for the buzzing in my ears.

I could feel the blood pulsing in my temples. My muscles throbbed. My heart raced.

I sat there for a long while. Just breathing . . . breathing.

Finally, I gripped the sides of the little car and hoisted myself up and onto the track. Brandon was already out of his car. He was running toward me with an angry expression on his face.

I started to call to him. But my whole body twisted in a violent shudder. I started to shake all over. My hands flew up wildly over my head.

I did a crazy dance. My arms and legs thrashed and shook. I dropped to my knees on the asphalt track.

"The shock . . . !" I gasped. "Too much! Can't . . . take . . . it! Oh, help! Help! Make it STOP!"

Brandon uttered a terrified cry. "Ray!" he screeched. He hurtled himself toward me. "Are you okay? Stop shaking! Can't you stop?"

He grabbed my shoulders and tried to hold me still.

I burst out laughing. "Gotcha," I said. "You fell for it, dude. I'm just kidding. I'm perfectly okay."

His mouth dropped open. He blinked his dark eyes several times. He still had hold of my shoulders. He gave me a hard shove that sent me toppling to my butt.

"You're a jerk, Ray," he growled.

"Hey — it was a joke!" I cried.

"But ... but why do you always like to scare me?"

"Because it's so easy," I said. I grabbed on to him and pulled myself to my feet.

"That ride was *horrible*!" Brandon said.

"It definitely needs work," I said. I looked around. "Where is that Horror? We have to get out of here."

I didn't see him anywhere. Did he just leave us in here?

We started to walk along the track. Our footsteps thudded loudly in the deep silence. "I think we came in over there," I said, pointing.

We heard a shout. Brandon and I both turned as a man came jogging after us.

He was big, with his huge stomach bouncing in front of him. He wore a loose-fitting pale blue sweatshirt pulled down over baggy brown pants.

I raised my eyes to his face — and uttered a sharp cry.

He didn't *have* a face!

No. Wait. I couldn't see his eyes, nose, or mouth — because his whole head was mirror glass. He leaned toward us, and I saw my reflection in his face!

We froze as he came bouncing toward us. He raised a hand in greeting. His hand was also mirror glass!

"He must be some kind of robot," Brandon whispered.

"No, I'm not," the man said. He had a high, croaky voice. He stopped right in front of us.

He turned his mirror face to me, then to my brother. The lights from the dome ceiling sparkled on his head. His neck was glass, as were both hands.

"Allow me to introduce myself," he said. "My name is Seymour Winn-Doe."

I pointed to his face. I could see my hand reflected back at me. "Are you wearing some kind of mirror mask?" I asked.

He shook his head. It sent rays of light sweeping across the floor.

"Is it painted on?" I asked.

He shook his head again. "No. I worked at a glass factory. There was a terrible accident."

Brandon and I both stared at him.

Was he serious?

"Reflect on that!" Winn-Doe exclaimed. He laughed a croaky laugh. He shrugged his wide shoulders. "I can only joke," he murmured. "What can I do? Gotta keep my sense of humor."

Was his body really damaged in a glass factory accident? I couldn't tell if he was for real or not. But the mirrored face and hands were way creepy.

"I was told you want to see something really scary," Winn-Doe said.

"Not really," Brandon replied.

"Yes, we do," I said. I tried to give Brandon a shove. But the big hulk didn't budge.

Winn-Doe motioned for us to follow him. "I just finished building a new attraction," he said.

15

"A Hall of Mirrors. When it opens, it will be the scariest thing in HorrorLand."

Brandon stopped walking. "Do we have to go?" he whispered.

I tried to tug him forward, but he was too strong for me. "We'll just look at it for a second," I said. "Then we'll go."

"Promise?" Brandon asked.

What a big baby!

Winn-Doe led us out of the bubble building and across the test area. I didn't see anyone else around. I was totally *pumped*. Brandon and I were getting a chance to see so many parts of the park that no one else got to see!

The sun had finally come out. The man's mirrored head reflected the bright sunlight.

He led us to a long, low building. It had a narrow door at one end and no windows. The front wall was painted black. I didn't see any sign saying what it was.

Winn-Doe unlocked the door and pulled it open. He motioned with a mirrored hand for us to go inside. "Enjoy it," he said. "I think you will find my mirrors are very special."

"Cool," I said. I stepped past him and started to enter.

But my brother hung back. "Is it — is it *dark* in there?" Brandon stammered.

"You'll see," Winn-Doe replied. He gave

Brandon a gentle push. Brandon bumped up behind me as we made our way inside.

I expected Winn-Doe to follow us in. Instead, I heard the door slam shut behind us. Then I heard the click of the lock.

The air inside the narrow building was hot and musty. I blinked in the darkness, waiting for a light to come on.

"What's up with this?" I whispered to Brandon. "It's pitch-black in here. I can't even *see* the mirrors!"

Brandon bumped me again. "I — I don't like this," he whispered back. "Why did he lock the door?"

Good question.

4

I felt a trickle of sweat run down my cheek. It had to be a hundred degrees in here. My throat suddenly felt tight and dry.

Brandon squeezed my arm. "Why aren't there any lights?" he asked. "Why isn't anything happening? Where did he go?"

"I — I don't know," I stammered. I took a deep breath and shouted, "Hey — is anyone here?"

I stuck my hands out in front of me. I could feel glass. Warm to the touch. But I couldn't see it.

"Let us out of here!" Brandon shouted. "Let us out!"

And then, dim lights flickered on somewhere above us.

I saw my face. My reflection. Staring back at me. Very dark. All shadows and black with no color at all.

Brandon stopped shouting. I saw him blinking

in the dim light. He reached out a big hand and rubbed it on the mirror in front of him.

I turned and gazed down the long, narrow aisle. I saw my reflection in mirror after mirror. Two rows of dark mirrors. A dozen Rays and Brandons. Maybe more, in front of us and behind us.

The dim light sent shadows over the glass. Our faces looked mysterious. Frightening. My eyes looked like deep, black holes. My mouth appeared jagged and torn.

I raised my right hand and watched the right hands go up in all the mirrors. I did a little dance, and the Ray reflections danced with me.

"What's so scary about this?" Brandon demanded. "What's the special part? It's just a bunch of mirrors. They aren't curved or twisted or anything."

"You're right," I said. I turned to him — and gasped. "Hey — where are you?"

"What do you mean, Ray?"

"I — I can't see you," I replied. My heart started to pound.

"Stop it, Ray," Brandon snapped. "You're not funny. I'm so sick of your dumb jokes."

"I'm not joking," I said. "Brandon, I really can't see you!"

"But I'm standing right next to you!" he cried.

I gazed into the mirrors. Yes. There he was. Standing beside me. His face twisted in an angry frown.

"I can see your reflections," I said. "But I can't see *you*."

"You jerk." Brandon gave me a hard shove that sent my shoulder crashing into a mirror. "See me *now*?"

"No," I told him. "I'm not joking, Brandon."

"Look," he said. "Look at my reflections. See me pointing at the mirror? See me getting ready to punch you in the stomach?"

"I . . . I see the reflection," I said. "But I can't see you standing next to me. I'm not joking, Brandon. I'm totally serious."

He turned away from the mirrors. There was a long silence.

He finally spoke. "Oh, wow," he said with a moan. "Oh, wow. Ray. Now I can't see you, either."

We were both silent for a long time.

"This has to be some kind of light trick," I murmured. "The lights up on the ceiling block us out somehow."

"But — that's impossible," Brandon answered in a whisper.

Then I looked down — and gasped again. "Oh, noo," I moaned. "Brandon, I can't see *myself*!"

I waved my hands in front of my face. I couldn't see them.

I saw them moving in the mirror in front of me. But I couldn't see my hands in front of me!

"I'm invisible, too!" Brandon cried. "Ray — help me. I'm invisible!"

"Somebody let us out of here!" I shouted. My voice came out hoarse and frightened. I started to pound on a mirror with both fists. "Let us out of here! Somebody — let us OUT!"

And then I stopped pounding. My words choked in my throat. And I staggered back as the reflections in the mirror began to move.

Brandon and me. Our reflections. All down the two long rows of mirrors, they tossed back their heads and began to laugh.

5

"AAAAIIIIIIIEEEE!"

I opened my mouth in a scream of horror that drowned out the crazy laughter from the mirrors.

Our reflections laughed and laughed. Cold, mechanical laughter. Cold and cruel.

I felt a stab of pain and realized Brandon was squeezing my arm. I couldn't see him. I couldn't see myself. But I felt his hand grabbing me in panic.

I stumbled back against a mirror. I pressed my hands over my ears, trying to shut out the wild laughter.

And suddenly the reflections all vanished. The mirrors went blank. Dark, empty mirrors.

No reflections. And no Brandon and me.

I stood there in silence. I realized I was holding my breath. I let it out in a long whoosh. My legs were trembling. I stared straight ahead at the dark mirror in front of me.

"Hey!" I uttered a startled shout as bright lights flashed on.

Blinking, I turned and saw Brandon. Yes! He was standing there, looking as shocked as I was.

We stared at each other for a long moment. There we were. Back. Under the bright lights. Our reflections bright in front of us.

The door swung open.

We raced each other, bumping, squeezing down the narrow aisle. Out into the daylight.

I struggled to catch my breath. The cool afternoon air felt good on my hot, sweaty face. "Yaaaaay!" I pumped my fists above my head.

I stopped when Winn-Doe appeared in our path. My reflection stared back at me from his mirrored face.

"You liked it?" he asked.

Brandon and I stared at him. We were both still breathing hard.

"How did you do that?" I finally found my voice. "Tell us! How did you make us invisible like that?"

"Yeah," Brandon chimed in. "How did you make our reflections laugh at us?"

Winn-Doe scratched his glassy head with a mirrored hand. "Huh? Do *what*?" he asked. "It's just a Hall of Mirrors."

"You turned us invisible," I said. "And you made our reflections laugh at us."

"What are you saying?" Winn-Doe replied. "That's impossible!"

I stared at him. My brain whirred. "You mean . . ." I started. "You mean you don't know about it? Really?"

"It's just mirrors," Winn-Doe said. "That's all. A long, dark room with mirrors."

"But . . ." Brandon started.

"Prove it to me," Winn-Doe said. He grabbed my hand and started to pull me back to the Hall of Mirrors. "Let's go back inside, guys. Prove it to me."

"No way!" I cried.

No way was I going back into that creepy little building!

"Brandon — run!" I cried. I swung my hand free of Winn-Doe's grip and took off.

Brandon came lumbering after me.

I didn't look back. Was Winn-Doe chasing after us? I didn't care. I just wanted to get away from him.

I pushed open the gate to the test area and burst back into the park. Brandon and I ran full speed into a crowd of people.

We ran until we were back in Zombie Plaza. I gazed all around at the shops and food stands. I nearly crashed into a drinks cart selling DEAD SKUNK & DIET DEAD SKUNK. TASTES GREAT IF YOU HOLD YOUR NOSE WHILE YOU DRINK.

24

"I think . . . I think he's coming after us." Brandon's voice cracked. His black hair was matted to his forehead with sweat. His chest heaved up and down.

I pointed. "We'll hide in that shop."

We dodged through the crowd. Up to the front door of a little store at the end of the row.

CHILLER HOUSE. That's what the sign above the door said. I saw skulls and funny dolls and other souvenirs in the front window.

I pulled open the door and bolted inside.

A bell rang overhead.

Brandon stumbled in after me.

We made our way to the back of the shop. I kept glancing at the door. No sign of Winn-Doe.

The shop was long and narrow. Cluttered shelves and display cases rose up on both sides of us.

I bumped into a wall display of brown shrunken heads. The heads bobbed and swayed as if they were alive.

"Check this out," Brandon said. He held up a building set for kids. Coffin Fun Kit. The box showed a little man lying in a handmade wooden coffin with his arms crossed over his chest.

"Sweet," I said.

I picked up a plastic snake. It was actually a candy dispenser. When you squeezed its jaws open, a piece of candy slid out.

25

"Awesome store," I muttered. I checked the door. Still no sign of Winn-Doe. Maybe we lost him.

"Whoa." I saw something way cool on a table across from me. A wooden ventriloquist's dummy. It wore a tight-fitting gray suit and polka dot bow tie. Its brown hair was painted on its head. Its glassy blue eyes appeared to stare up at me.

It had an ugly, totally evil grin on its painted red lips.

"Brandon, check out this awesome dummy," I said. My brother dropped what he was looking at and came over.

I reached for the dummy and started to lift it into my arms.

Before I could pick it up, the dummy opened its mouth and shouted: *"Get your clammy hands off me!"*

"Hey!" I uttered a cry. I jumped back and fell onto Brandon.

An old man popped up behind the dummy. He had a shiny forehead with thinning white hair combed straight back. He wore weird-looking square glasses at the end of his nose. And he was dressed in a brown suit and vest that looked like they came from an old movie.

He held the dummy up in his hands. "Did you think Slappy here was talking?" he asked.

"Well . . ." I started. "I was a little surprised —"

The man laughed. A gold tooth sparkled on the side of his mouth. "I confess. I did it," he said. He set the dummy down on the counter behind him.

"Welcome to Chiller House." He waved his hand around the shop. I noticed that his shirt cuff was ruffled. "My name is Jonathan Chiller," he said. "Do you like Slappy?"

"Yes," I said. "Is he very expensive?"

"Not very," Chiller replied.

"You don't want him!" Brandon said. He pushed me away from the dummy. "He's too ugly and evil looking."

Chiller snickered. "He *does* have an evil grin — doesn't he?"

"I think he's cool," I said. "Maybe I'll start a dummy collection."

I collect a lot of stuff. Dad says I have the collecting bug. That makes it sound like a disease. But I think it's fun.

I have a skateboard collection, and a Transformers collection, and a baseball card collection, and a cereal box collection. And a lot of others.

I gazed at the grinning dummy. I pictured six or seven dummies like him sitting around in my room.

"Don't buy it, Ray," Brandon said, tugging my arm. "Really. I don't like it."

"It's not for you — it's for me," I said.

"But I'll see it every time I go in your room," Brandon said. "It will give me nightmares. You *know* I'm afraid of puppets and dummies."

"That's way dumb," I said. "Get over it."

Brandon pulled me toward the door. "Come on, Ray. That weird mirror guy is gone. Let's get out of here."

I could see that my big little brother was really afraid of the dummy. *I have to help the poor guy get over his fears*, I decided.

"I'll buy the dummy," I said to Chiller.

The old man's eyes twinkled behind the square glasses. "Very good. Slappy is yours. Come up front."

He picked up the dummy and carried it to the cash register at the counter. I followed after him.

Brandon grabbed my shoulder and spun me around. "Please —" he whined. "Please don't buy that thing, Ray. It's too creepy. Remember that movie you made me watch? The one with the dummy that comes to life and kills all those people?"

I laughed. "Yeah. That was funny. Awesome movie."

Then I remembered how angry Mom and Dad were at me for making Brandon watch that film. He had nightmares and had to sleep in their bed for a week!

"Dummies don't come alive in real life," I told Brandon. "So grow up."

"Please —" Brandon whined. "This one is so totally creepy."

I stepped up to the counter. "Don't listen to my brother. I'll take the dummy," I told Jonathan Chiller.

Chiller opened a drawer and pulled out a little green-and-purple doll. He held it up. It looked just like the Horrors who work in HorrorLand.

He tucked the little figure into the pocket of Slappy's jacket. "Take a little Horror home with you," Chiller said.

"We don't want it!" Brandon cried.

I ignored him. I reached for my money. "How much is it?" I asked.

Chiller waved a hand. "No. Don't pay me now," he said. He lifted the dummy into my arms. "You can pay me next time."

Huh? Next time?

What does he mean by that?

"Let's go," Brandon said. He kept shaking his head unhappily. "Mom and Dad are waiting, Ray. They're not going to be happy about that dummy."

"Don't be a total jerk," I said. I flung the dummy over my shoulder. Then I thanked Jonathan Chiller and followed Brandon back out onto Zombie Plaza.

The park was crowded. A Horror walked past with dozens of black helium balloons bobbing over his head. All the balloons in HorrorLand were black.

"Want a balloon?" I asked Brandon. "Oh, wait. You're probably scared of balloons."

"Don't be mean to me," Brandon pouted. He stuck out his bottom lip. "Don't make fun of me,

Ray. You'll be sorry about that dummy. You really will."

We walked toward the hotel. The dummy bounced on my shoulder. Brandon had his pouty face on the whole way.

We were almost to the hotel when the dummy tilted its head toward Brandon. And it said in a hoarse whisper: *"You'll be sorry, punk!"*

Brandon punched me in the back. "Stop it, Ray. That's not funny. Stop it!"

I turned to him. "Stop what?" I asked. "I didn't do anything."

"Stop trying to scare me," Brandon said. "You made the dummy talk. I *know* you did!"

I squinted hard at him. "Huh? *Me?* Are you *crazy*?"

PART TWO

Back home *two days* early.

That's right. Mom and Dad cut our HorrorLand visit short. Why? Three guesses.

Brandon. Brandon. Brandon.

My big, hulking little brother was too scared of everything. So we had to come home.

You know how to spell his name? A-N-N-O-Y-I-N-G.

A few days later, I woke up early. I don't know why. It was a Saturday morning. I usually sleep late. But that day, I woke up before everyone else.

I opened one eye and saw Slappy staring at me from the little rocking chair I put him in next to my bedroom window. Chuckling to myself, I picked him up and tiptoed out of my room.

I crept silently down the hall. The floorboards felt cold under my bare feet. The house was silent. I could hear the refrigerator humming downstairs.

Brandon sleeps with his door shut tight. He's afraid of wild animals or werewolves or a killer bat bursting in while he's asleep. He also has two night-lights. Because one isn't bright enough.

Carefully, I turned the doorknob and pushed open his bedroom door. It creaked a little. I peeked in. No. It didn't wake him.

His jeans and T-shirts from the whole week were piled in a heap in the middle of the floor. His SpongeBob SquarePants pillow lay on the floor beside his bed.

I saw his paint jars and other supplies lined up neatly on his art table. My brother is a pretty good artist. He likes to paint and make sculptures and papier-mâché animals and stuff.

Silently, I stepped into his room. Carrying Slappy in front of me, I tiptoed up to his bed.

Brandon was sound asleep on his side, one arm tucked under his pillow.

Holding my breath, I crept behind him. Then I lowered myself to the floor.

I ducked real low and raised the dummy's head over the bed. I brought it real close to Brandon's pillow, just a few inches from his nose.

And then I screamed at the top of my lungs in a high, shrill voice: "KILL! KILL! KILL!"

I'll never forget the look on my brother's face as he woke up. Opened his eyes — and saw the dummy in his face, shrieking at him.

"KILL! KILL! KILL!"

What a riot!

Brandon tried to scream. But he choked instead, and a gob of drool dripped down his chin.

He leaped from the bed. Got all tangled in his covers. Hit the floor on his elbows and knees.

Then he started to scream for Mom and Dad. He pulled himself up and tore out of his room. I heard his heavy, thudding footsteps as he ran screaming down the hall.

A few seconds later, he was crying and whining in Mom and Dad's room. Quietly, I picked up Slappy and ran down the hall back to my room.

I dropped Slappy back into his rocking chair. Then I jumped back into bed, pulled the covers over me, and pretended to be asleep.

Mom and Dad came stomping into my room.

"Ray — we need to talk to you!"

"Why did you scare your little brother again?"

I pretended to wake up slowly. I yawned and blinked my eyes. "Huh? Scared who?" I asked in a sleepy voice.

But they weren't fooled.

"We heard you running back to your room, Ray," Mom said.

Dad picked up Slappy and shook him. "Why did you buy this, Ray?" he asked angrily. "Just to torture Brandon?"

"You know he's frightened of puppets and things," Mom said.

I saw Brandon back in my doorway, head down, whimpering softly to himself. He was making a big deal of it. He wasn't really that scared.

"Is that why you bought this ugly doll?" Dad demanded. "To scare your brother?"

"No," I said. "I'm going to start collecting dummies. I think they're cool."

"Don't you have enough collections?" Mom asked. "You have so many collections, I can't ever clean this room!" She stared hard at the flowerpots holding my toadstool collection on the windowsill.

I climbed out of bed, crossed the room, and took the dummy from Dad's hands. "I'm going to learn how to throw my voice," I said.

"Just don't scare Brandon with it," Dad said. He crossed his arms over his pajama shirt and gave me the fish eye. He thinks that makes him look angry. But it just makes him look weird.

"You really want to have that New Year's Eve party — right?" Mom said. "You and Elena?"

"She's his girlfriend," Brandon said from the doorway.

"She is NOT!" I screamed. "You're just jealous because you don't have any friends!"

"Brandon has lots of friends," Mom said. "Don't change the subject, Ray. If you and Elena want

38

to have that New Year's party, you've got to change your attitude."

"Okay. It's changed," I said.

Elena and I really wanted to have this party for our whole class. That's because adults always forget about kids on New Year's Eve. They leave us home watching TV. And there's nowhere for us to hang out.

Elena and I had this great idea for a party, which is going to make us totally popular with everybody. And that's a *good* thing — right?

"Mom, we *have* to have the party," I said. "Everyone in my class is counting on us."

"Well, you have to earn it," Mom said. "First, I want you to make a list of New Year's resolutions."

"Good idea," Dad said. "Make a list of all the ways you're going to be better and nicer next year."

I stared at them both. "You're serious about this?"

They nodded.

"And what should number one on your list be?" Mom asked.

I took a wild guess. "That I won't scare Brandon?"

They nodded again.

I lifted Slappy in front of me. I made his mouth move up and down. And I made him say, *"I'm nice now! I'm nice now!"*

Mom and Dad laughed. But Brandon stood there and glared angrily at me.

After breakfast, I waited for Elena to come over. I went up to my room to make my list of New Year's resolutions. How would I change for the better next year?

I sat down at my computer and began to type:

1. I won't scare Brandon too much.
2. I'll help out more around the house when I can.
3. I'll try my best to keep my collections neater.

These were pretty good. But I needed a few more.

I was struggling to think of a fourth one when Brandon wandered into my room. His eyes were on the dummy propped up in the rocking chair in front of the window.

"Don't get mad or anything," Brandon started. "I just want to ask you a favor."

"Okay. Shoot," I said.

"Would you get rid of that dummy?" Brandon asked. "It really scares me. Seriously."

"Ooh, seriously," I said, mimicking his voice. "That's a big word for you."

"Please —" Brandon said.

"I've got an idea," I told him. "Go make your own list of New Year's resolutions. Number one should be to grow up and be brave next year."

Brandon opened his mouth to reply. But before he could speak, we heard a loud, angry *YOWWWWWWLLLL* from the window.

I leaped to my feet. "Oh, wow," I said. "That was SLAPPY!"

Brandon gasped. His eyes bulged and he went pale.

I laughed. "You geek. That wasn't the dummy."

I ran to the window and peered down to the side of our yard.

Brandon didn't move from beside my bed. He hugged himself and stared hard at Slappy.

I pointed out the window. "Look. Come here, Brandon. Look down there. It's Bobo, the Willards' cat."

Brandon shuffled to the window and gazed down. Bobo, a small orange-and-white cat, pawed at the Willards' back door. He uttered another yowl. I think he wanted back inside.

I slapped my brother on the back. "Way to go, baby. You were terrified by a little pussycat."

Brandon pushed my arm away. "Awww, big deal. I still don't like that dummy," he snapped.

Elena walked into the room, shaking her head. "Brandon, you're a big, strong guy," she said. "You're the biggest kid in the fourth grade, right? You shouldn't be afraid of little kittens."

Brandon's face turned bright red. He wasn't happy that Elena overheard everything. I think he kind of has a crush on her.

"I'm not afraid of kittens," he muttered through clenched teeth. He pushed his black hair off his forehead. Then he turned and stomped out of my room.

Elena laughed. She has a high-pitched giggle. My mom says Elena has a face that always seems to be laughing.

She has wavy brown hair that she usually ties back in a ponytail. Green eyes and a stub of a nose with tiny freckles on her cheeks. When she smiles, her two front teeth poke out of her mouth. But she refuses to get braces.

Elena is short and thin like me. Today she wore a big yellow-and-black smiley face T-shirt pulled down over faded jeans with tears at both knees.

We've been friends since we were babies. We didn't have a choice. Our parents all went to school together. They are all best friends.

"So?" Elena said, plopping down on the edge of my bed. "What about the New Year's Eve party?"

"What about it?" I asked.

43

"Can we start getting your basement ready?" She picked up my pillow and began squeezing it between her hands.

"Why are you doing that?" I asked.

She shrugged. "No reason." She tossed the pillow at me. I ducked, and it bounced off my desk.

"Hey, I bought you a Christmas present," she said.

I stared at her. "Really?"

She nodded. "You know your family is coming to my house to exchange presents this year. It's our turn."

I picked up the pillow and heaved it back at her. "What did you get me?" I asked.

She giggled. "I can't tell. It's a surprise."

"Give me a hint," I said.

She thought for a moment. "Well, it's for your collection of old bottles."

"Bet I can guess," I said. "Is it an old bottle?"

"Not telling." She jumped to her feet. "Whoa. What's *that* ugly thing?"

She walked to the window and lifted Slappy from his rocking chair. "Hey, he's heavy."

"That's Slappy," I said. "I might start a collection of old dummies."

Elena sniffed. "Yuck. He smells kind of ratty. You should have his suit cleaned."

"I don't think it comes off," I said. "It's sewn on or something."

44

"He's totally nasty looking," she said. "Is Brandon afraid of him?"

"Three guesses," I said.

Elena dropped the dummy back into the chair. She reached into the jacket pocket and pulled something out. "Ray, what's this?"

"It's a tiny Horror," I said. "You know. Those dudes from HorrorLand."

"Wait. There's something else in the pocket," Elena said. She slid her fingers in and pulled out a folded-up sheet of paper.

"I didn't see that," I said. "What is it? Instructions?" I grabbed for it, but Elena swung it away from me.

She turned her back and unfolded the paper. Then she started to read what was written there:

"'Hello. My name is Slappy. I can be your friend. Just read these words aloud, and I will come to life. We can have a lot of fun together.'"

"Weird," I said. "Totally weird."

I leaned over Elena's shoulder and studied the paper. I saw a bunch of strange, foreign-looking words at the bottom.

"What language is that?" I murmured.

"I don't know. Let's try it," Elena said. She giggled. "Let's bring the dummy to life!"

She lowered her eyes to the page and began to read. . . .

"'*Karru . . . marri . . . odonna . . .*'"

"NO! STOP!"

Brandon came diving into the room. "Stop it, Elena!" he screeched.

He swiped the paper away from her before she could finish reading the six words.

"Brandon — what is your *problem*?" Elena cried.

"Give it back to her," I said.

Brandon shook his head. "No way." He swung the paper behind his back.

"You don't think the dummy will really come to life — do you?" Elena demanded.

Brandon didn't budge.

"That's way stupid," Elena said. "It's just a painted doll, Brandon. You can't be that big a 'fraidy cat."

Brandon blushed again.

I lifted Slappy into my arms. "Here. You hold him. You'll see. He isn't scary."

46

I pushed the dummy toward Brandon. But he pushed it back.

"Just leave me alone," he muttered. He folded up the paper and jammed it back into Slappy's jacket pocket. "And stop making fun of me!"

Elena and I couldn't help it. We both burst out laughing. We didn't want to be mean. I guess it was just the frightened look on Brandon's face.

My poor brother blushed even redder. "You'll be sorry," he muttered.

Suddenly, his eyes bulged. He made a choking sound.

"Brandon — what's wrong?" I cried.

"The dummy! It — it —" He began pointing at it, furiously jabbing his finger toward it.

"The dummy's eyes! I saw them *blink*!" Brandon screamed. "He's alive! He's *alive*!"

He whirled around, screaming — and went running full speed out of my room.

10

Elena frowned at me. "*You* did that — didn't you, Ray? You made the eyes blink?"

I nodded. A grin spread over my face. "Yeah. I did it."

I heard Brandon's heavy footsteps as he ran into his room and slammed the door shut.

"See? You pull this string," I said. I turned the dummy around so that Elena could see. Then I made the eyes blink a few times. I could also make them move from side to side. It looked just like the dummy was glancing around the room.

Elena grabbed the dummy's wooden hand and shook hands with it. "Way to go, dummy," she said. "You sure have Ray's little brother totally freaked."

The dummy grinned its evil red-lipped grin at her.

"Brandon deserves it," I said. "The big wimp totally ruined my trip to HorrorLand."

"I know, I know." Elena said with a groan. "He made you come home two days early. You told me that a hundred times."

"It's still true," I said. I dropped Slappy onto his chair.

"Are we going to make plans for the party or what?" Elena said.

I started to answer, but Mom came bursting into the room.

Mom is a big, tall person like Brandon. And she can come on strong when she's angry. Sometimes Dad calls her Hurricane. I guess because she can rush at you like a powerful wind.

Well, she was definitely in hurricane mode right now.

"Did you scare your brother *again* with that ugly dummy?" she shouted. Her dark eyes flared. She stopped and tapped one foot on the floor rapidly.

Tap tap tap tap.

"I didn't do anything!" I cried. "I just made his eyes blink. How scary is *that*?"

"Well, put that dummy away," Mom said. She crossed her arms tightly in front of her. "Put it away. I don't want to hear any more about you scaring Brandon."

"Okay," I muttered. "You won't hear any more."

"Don't be smart," Mom snapped. She turned to Elena. "Tell him to be nice to his brother."

"Ray, be nice to your brother," Elena said.

Mom rolled her eyes. "You're as bad as Ray."

"No, I'm not," Elena said. "I'm nice to Brandon. I think he's cute."

"Cute?" I cried. "He's a *hulk*!"

Mom's expression changed. "Brandon *is* cute," she said. "He's sweet, too. Know what he's doing right now? He's in his room, making his own Christmas wrapping paper with his paints."

"Big whoop," I muttered.

"You *know* he's a wonderful artist," Mom said. "I want you to stop picking on him. And be nice to him."

"Okay, okay," I said. I walked over to my computer and pointed to the screen. "Check it out, Mom. It's my number one New Year's resolution."

I read it to her. The one about how I was going to be nicer to Brandon when I could.

Mom squinted at the screen. Then she turned to me. "I hope you mean these resolutions," she said. "I hope you stick to them. If you don't . . . no New Year's party. I'm serious."

"Don't worry," Elena chimed in. "I'll *make* him stick to them, Mrs. Gordon. We really want that party."

The phone rang. Mom hurried downstairs to answer it.

50

Elena crossed the room and stepped up to me. She snapped my nose with two fingers. "Don't mess up, Ray," she said.

"*Ow.*" I rubbed my nose. "How much do I hate it when you do that?"

She snapped my nose again. "A lot?"

"Go away," I said. "You're too violent."

She laughed. "I have to go home anyway. But remember — everyone is counting on us to have this party."

"No problem," I muttered. "Catch you later."

After she left, I sat at my computer. I tried to think of more New Year's resolutions. But I couldn't come up with any.

I turned and gazed at the dummy. I walked over and picked him up.

The glassy eyes seemed to stare at me. I saw a tiny chip in the dummy's lower lip.

I reached into the jacket pocket and pulled out the sheet of paper. I put the dummy back on his chair. I unfolded the paper and stared at the six strange, foreign words.

Should I read them out loud?

Why not?

I held the paper in one hand and started to read . . .

"*'Karru . . . marri . . . odonna . . .'*"

I admit it. As I slowly read the words, a shiver of fear ran down my back.

"*'. . . loma . . . molonu . . .'*"

"Ray — come downstairs!"

Dad's shout came before I could read the last word.

"Coming!" I called. I tucked the paper back into Slappy's pocket and hurried down.

Dad was waiting with his parka on. "Come with me to the hardware store," he said. "It might snow. I want to buy bags of salt for the driveway and front walk."

"No problem," I said.

I wanted to show Dad how helpful I could be. I raced to get my coat.

I felt pretty good.

The horror didn't start until the next day.

11

"Whoa. These are heavy," I said.

Dad lifted a paint can off the pile. "Hold it by the handle," he said. "Then put a hand under the bottom."

He carried the can to the wall and set it down next to some others. "I'll do the gallon cans," he said. "You carry the half gallons."

We were in the basement, clearing a space for my New Year's party. I didn't count them. But there were paint cans stacked high all over the room. Dozens and dozens of paint cans to move out of the way.

My dad had a paint store in town. But it went out of business a few months ago. Dad is storing his paint cans down here until he figures out what to do with them.

"We'll make a wall of cans over here," Dad said. "And we can stack some more over by the washing machine."

I lifted a can in each hand and staggered

toward the wall. "Wish Elena was here," I said with a groan. "She's missing out on the fun part."

"Did you call her?" Dad asked.

I nodded. "Yeah. Her mom said she had a tennis lesson."

Dad tilted a can of paint in his hands and read the label. "This is good stuff," he said. "Maybe I'll save it and paint the kitchen."

I started to say something — but stopped.

A shrill scream of horror made me drop the paint cans I was carrying.

Another high, shrill scream rang down from upstairs.

"Hey — that's Brandon!" I cried.

I started for the basement stairs — stumbled over a paint can and banged my knee as I went down. Dad reached the stairs first. He went roaring up them two at a time.

Rubbing my knee, I followed him to Brandon's room.

Mom was already there. Her eyes were wide. She had her hands pressed against her cheeks. Her face was very red.

"Ray — how could you *do* this?" she said through clenched teeth.

"Huh?"

I gazed around the room. My heart skipped a beat. I made a choking sound.

Brandon's whole room had been *trashed*!

12

Brandon sat hunched on his bed. He had his hands over his face. His big shoulders were heaving up and down. He was sobbing loudly.

"I — I —" I stuttered.

I blinked at the mess. Shreds of Brandon's homemade wrapping paper were tossed everywhere. On the desk. On the floor. All over his bed.

The wrapping paper had been ripped to pieces. Strips of it, still wet, were stuck to his mirror and the wall.

The paint jars rolled on their sides. Thick puddles of red and blue paint spread over his white shag rug. His bedspread was smeared with yellow paint.

"How could you? How could you?" Mom repeated, staring hard at me. When she pulled her hands away, I could see tears running down her face.

"Ray, how could you do something so horrible

55

to your brother?" she demanded. She didn't yell. Her voice was a raspy whisper.

Dad had his hands balled into tight fists. He looked kind of sick, like he might puke. He shook his head sadly and didn't look at me.

"I — I didn't," I choked out.

Brandon lifted his head. Tears filled his eyes. He made a sound like *glub glub*. Then he wailed, "I worked *so hard* on my wrapping paper!"

He started to sob some more.

I had this heavy feeling in my stomach, like I'd just swallowed a huge rock. Brandon is such a big guy, I always forget he's only nine.

Dad grabbed my shoulder. "I'm very disappointed in you, Ray."

"But I didn't do it!" I screamed. "I swear! I didn't! I didn't! I didn't do it!"

Dad let go of my shoulder and took a step back. He and Mom both glared at me.

"Don't lie," Dad said. "Don't make it worse by lying."

Brandon uttered a loud sob. He used his bedspread to wipe the tears off his face.

I started to cross the room. My shoes stuck in shreds of wet wrapping paper.

"I didn't do this!" I cried. "Don't keep staring at me like that. I didn't do it — really!"

"Ray, stop," Mom said softly. "Just stop."

Dad shook his head again. "You really don't

expect us to believe that the dummy made this mess — *do* you?"

"Huh? Dummy?"

Dad pointed to the corner of the room by Brandon's closet.

"Oh . . . noooo," I moaned.

Slappy sat on the floor in the corner, propped up against the wall.

I took a few steps toward him.

He had shreds of wrapping paper in his lap. And as I came closer, I saw spots of red and yellow paint on his hands.

The dummy grinned up at me, as if pleased with himself.

"But — but —" I sputtered. "How did he get in here?" I turned to my parents. "I didn't put him there. I swear! I didn't do this!"

13

What a horrible mess. Of *course* Mom and Dad didn't believe me.

I wouldn't believe me, either, if I was them.

How did that dummy get there? And how could he do all this damage?

Karru marri odonna . . . The strange foreign words slipped into my head. The words that were supposed to bring the dummy to life.

But that was *crazy*. Ridiculous.

I stared down at the dummy. He grinned back at me. His glassy eyes appeared to flash with excitement.

No. No way.

I didn't even finish reading the weird words out loud. I never read the last word.

Besides, dummies don't come to life. That's only in dumb horror movies.

"Ray, you'll clean everything up," Dad said in a soft, low voice, a voice that meant business.

"Right," I said.

"And you'll put that dummy away," Mom added. "Somewhere we can't see it."

"Right," I repeated.

"And you will promise that you will *never* try to scare your brother again," Mom said.

"Never," I murmured.

I glanced at the dummy's smiling face. I blinked. Had the grin grown wider?

"Now, apologize to Brandon," Dad said.

Brandon wiped his face on the bedspread again. He scowled at me.

"But I can't apologize for something I didn't do!" I said.

"Ray, do you want to have your New Year's Eve party?" Mom asked.

I nodded. "Yeah."

"Then apologize to Brandon."

"Brandon, I apologize," I said.

What else could I do?

"I'm very very very sorry this happened," I told Brandon.

Brandon made that *glub glub* sound again. He nodded his head. I guess that meant he forgave me.

"Get this room cleaned up, and we won't talk about this again," Dad said.

"Good," I muttered. I hoisted Slappy onto my shoulder and carried him to the door. "This is the end of it," I said.

Wow. Was I wrong!

*   *   *

I tossed Slappy onto the floor of my closet. His head clonked hard on the floorboards. I shoved him under my shirts.

Mom and Dad were still down the hall in Brandon's room. I closed the door to my bedroom. I had to think.

My brain was doing flip-flops. My stomach still felt like a rock.

What exactly was going on here?

I was the only one in the Gordon family who knew I was innocent.

No way could I prove it. The vote was three-to-one that I was guilty.

So who trashed Brandon's bedroom and ripped up his wrapping paper? Yes, Slappy had paint on his hands and shreds of paper all over him. But I just wasn't ready to believe that the dummy came to life and did all that.

I pulled out the carton I keep my bottle collection in. Then I sat down and studied some of the old bottles.

That's what I do sometimes when I need to calm down. There's something about the cool smoothness of the glass and the nice shapes. My bottles always make me feel better.

Sure, it sounds weird. Well, lots of kids think I'm weird because I collect things like old bottles.

I guess that's one reason the New Year's Eve

party was so important to me. I really wanted to show kids that I'm a good guy. I've never been very popular. I guess I was hoping the party would help me out with that.

A knock on my door interrupted my thoughts.

"Ray? Are you forgetting something?" Mom called. "Are you forgetting the cleanup in Brandon's room?"

"Coming," I said. "I'll make it like new. Promise!"

As I started for the door, I glimpsed Slappy's shoes poking out of my closet. His legs were half-way out the closet doorway.

Was that the way I left him? Did he *move*?

14

The next day, Elena came over to help decorate the basement for our party. She wore a baggy gray sweatshirt and sweatpants. "Ready to go to work," she said.

Mom gave us lunch first. Big stacks of pancakes drowned in maple syrup. "This will give you strength to work," Mom said. "Are all the paint cans out of the way?"

"Most of them," I said with a mouthful of pancake.

Elena laughed. "You have a syrup mustache."

I tried to lick it off. "Mmmmm. Tastes even better if you lick it off your face."

"You're gross," Elena said. She nabbed a pancake off my stack and dropped it onto her plate.

Mom thought it was funny, so I didn't do anything about it. Mom thinks everything Elena does is cute or funny.

She's wrong.

Later, the two of us were sweeping the

basement floor with long-handled brooms. The floor had big balls of dust scattered over it. There were still a few paint cans to lug to the side.

"Does your Mom have any old rugs we could put on the floor?" Elena asked.

I shrugged. "How should I know?"

"Don't be such a grouch," she said. She swept a cloud of dust at me. "We want it to look like a party — right? How many pizzas is your dad buying?"

"He said one pizza for every three kids," I answered. "About three slices a kid."

"Nice," Elena said. "How come you're being so weird, Ray? I thought you were *psyched* about this party. Why are you acting like your puppy died?"

I shrugged again. I really didn't want to tell her about the whole thing with Slappy and Brandon's room.

"Things are kind of weird around here," I said.

"So what else is new?" she snapped.

That's when we heard the scream. Another frightened howl from upstairs.

"Brandon!" I gasped. I tossed the broom down and started for the stairs.

"What's he screaming about?" Elena called.

"I — I don't know," I said. I grabbed the metal banister and started to pull myself up the steps. "It doesn't sound good."

Where were Mom and Dad? Could they hear Brandon's high screams?

I bolted through the kitchen to the living room, then hurtled up the stairs to Brandon's room.

"What's up? What's wrong?" I shouted breathlessly.

The first thing I saw was Slappy.

The dummy was perched on top of Brandon's dresser with his legs dangling down the front. The top drawer was open. The dummy grinned at me with his mouth hanging open.

Elena stopped in the doorway. "Brandon? What's wrong?" she cried.

Brandon stood in the center of the room. His face was red and his eyes were wide with fright. "Look!" he cried. "Look in there!" He pointed frantically to the dresser.

"How did the dummy get out of my closet?" I demanded. "Is that what you're screaming about?"

"L-look in the top drawer," Brandon stammered. "My T-shirt drawer. Look at it!"

"Huh?" Elena and I stepped up to the dresser. "Oh, wow."

What was that dark brown gunk poured all over my brother's shirts?

It looked like motor oil.

I dipped a finger in it. Sticky and thick. I sniffed it.

"That's no way to find out," Elena said. She

dipped a finger in. Then she tasted it carefully with the tip of her tongue.

She made a disgusted face. She swallowed once. Twice.

"Ohhh, yuck. What is it?" I asked.

Elena grabbed her throat. "Can't breathe . . ." she choked out. "Poison! It's *poison*!"

15

"Elena! NOOOO!" I screamed.

She laughed. "Kidding. It's maple syrup."

"Huh? Maple syrup?"

Brandon nodded. "Maple syrup. Look at it. Poured all over the drawer. My — my shirts are all *ruined*!"

I gazed at Slappy. I saw dark syrup stains on the sleeve of his jacket. I stepped back. A thick river of syrup dripped all the way down the front of Brandon's dresser.

Brandon lurched forward and gave me a hard bump with his chest. He caught me off balance. I staggered back and toppled onto his bed.

The big hulk came charging at me. But Elena moved quickly to step between us.

"Why are you doing this to me?" he cried. "Why are you being such a jerk?"

Mom burst into the room. She had a stack of clean bath towels in her arms. "Why did Ray do *what*?" she asked. "What's all the racket in here?"

"He poured syrup in my dresser!" Brandon cried. "And he — he put that dummy up there."

Mom dropped the towels beside me on the bed. She brushed past Elena. Stepped up to the dresser and peered into the open drawer.

"Oh, my goodness. My goodness." She shook her head hard, as if trying to shake the whole thing away. "My goodness. Your shirts. Oh, it's all so sticky. What a mess!"

She spun away from the dresser and narrowed her eyes at me. "Why did you do this? Have you totally lost your mind?"

I jumped to my feet. The stack of towels fell to the floor. "I — I didn't," I stammered. My voice cracked. I cleared my throat. "I didn't do this! I swear!"

Mom started angrily stamping one foot on the floor. "Don't lie, Ray. Just tell us why you did it. What is going on with you?"

"Nothing!" I cried. "Nothing is going on with me. Mom, I'm telling the truth. I didn't bring the dummy in here. And I didn't pour syrup in Brandon's drawer."

"Ray was with me in the basement the whole time," Elena said.

"I should cancel your party right now," Mom said.

"Mom, please —"

"All my T-shirts are in that drawer!" Brandon wailed. "Now I have no shirts. What am I supposed to wear?"

"We'll find something of your dad's," Mom told him. "The syrup will come out in the wash. Don't worry. Your shirts will be good as new."

"Yuck. I don't want them anymore!" Brandon cried. "He hates me, Mom! Ray *hates* me!"

"Not true!" I shouted. "No way. That dummy —"

I glared angrily at Slappy. His head had tilted to one side. One shoe dangled down into the open drawer.

Mom stepped forward and put her hands on my shoulders. "Ray?" She brought her face down close to mine. "Stop. Take a breath. We are not going to believe that the dummy did this. So do not even start."

"But, Mom —"

"We live in the real world, Ray," she said softly. Her eyes burned into mine without blinking. "Do you agree? We don't live in a fantasy world."

"I didn't do it," I said. "That's all I can say."

"Well, you're grounded." She let go of me and stood up tall. "You're grounded, and I don't want to see that dummy out of the closet again."

"Okay," I murmured. No point in arguing.

"Maybe you can think real hard," Mom said,

"and figure out why you want to scare Brandon with that dummy."

"But —"

"And when you can explain it, then you won't be grounded anymore," Mom said.

"And . . . what about the New Year's Eve party?" Elena asked.

"Canceled," Mom said. "Forget about it."

Elena let out a cry. "No! Please! Give Ray one more chance! Just one! Please!"

Mom squinted at me, thinking hard. "Okay. I shouldn't — but one more chance. One more crazy incident — just one more — and the party is canceled," Mom said. "And no pleading or begging will change my mind."

I apologized again. I didn't know what else to do.

I carried the dummy back to my room. I shoved it back into the closet. Then I slammed the door shut.

Elena plopped down on my desk chair. She undid her ponytail and shook her brown hair out. She sighed loudly.

"You don't believe me, either — do you?" I said.

"I know what you're doing," she said softly. "And you're going to ruin our party."

"I'm not doing anything," I argued.

"You're trying to pay Brandon back for spoiling your trip to HorrorLand," Elena said.

"Not true!" I said. Suddenly, I remembered the words on that folded-up piece of paper. "Elena — listen to me. You know those weird words that are supposed to bring Slappy to life? Well . . . I read them."

She squinted at me. "Really?"

"Well . . . I didn't read them all," I said. "I only read *most* of them. But maybe that's enough to bring him to life."

Elena jumped to her feet. She tied her pony-tail back up. "I'm leaving."

"No. Listen," I said. "The dummy —"

She shook her head. "Ray, let's say the dummy came to life. Why is it only doing bad things to Brandon? Answer *that*!"

"Well . . ."

"Bye." She stomped out the door. She turned in the hall. "Just don't do any more tricks with the dummy, okay? I really want to have the party."

What could I say? Even my best friend didn't believe me.

I listened to her clomp down the stairs. Then I heard the front door slam shut behind her.

I paced back and forth in my room for a while. My brain was spinning. But I couldn't come up with any ideas to prove to everyone I was telling the truth.

Still thinking hard, I went down to the kitchen for a snack. I tore open a couple of pudding

70

containers and licked the pudding out like a dog. Then I poured myself a tall glass of milk.

I carried the milk up to my room. Stepped inside — and let out a scream. "Oh, nooo!"

Slappy was sitting cross-legged on my bed.

16

Was I frightened?

Three guesses — and they're all yes.

That night, I climbed into bed and pulled the covers up to my chin. I thought about Brandon and his night-lights. Maybe it wasn't such a bad idea.

Snow swirled outside my bedroom window. The wind made a creepy whistling sound. Moonlight through the whirling snow sent weird shadows dancing over the wall.

Slappy was on the floor in the back of my closet. I made sure the closet door was closed — and locked. But I still didn't feel safe.

I had the terrifying feeling he could find a way out of the closet whenever he wanted. What would he do next? Was he wrecking Brandon's room to get me in trouble?

I pressed my hands over my ears. The wind was howling like a wild animal now. My window-pane rattled and shook.

I kept glancing across the room to the closet door. I pictured it swinging open. And the dummy staggering out on its flimsy legs.

That's crazy, I told myself.

I shut my eyes tight. Pulled the covers higher. I opened my mouth in a long yawn.

Yes, I was tired. I needed to sleep. But how could I shut off my brain?

I kept thinking about the horrible things that happened to Brandon in his room. Even more horrible was the fact that my parents thought I did it. No one believed me when I swore it wasn't me.

I admit it. I was hurt. It hurts to have your whole family think you're some kind of wacko criminal.

Even Elena. Even my best friend thought I did those awful things to Brandon. She even dreamed up some kind of crazy reason about how I was doing it for revenge.

That hurts, too, when your best friend thinks you're a liar.

Mom always says I'm the sensitive one in the family. I don't really know what she means. I don't know if I'm sensitive or not. But I don't want my parents and my best friend to hate me and think I'm a total jerk.

I jumped at a loud, rattling sound. The closet door? No. Just the wind banging the windowpane.

Maybe I should get rid of the dummy, I thought. *It's only caused me trouble.*

I could put it in a big trash bag and drop it in a garbage can beside the garage.

But what if it really IS alive?

That thought sent a hard shiver down my whole body. Even under the covers I was trembling. I could feel my heart racing in my chest.

"I'll never get to sleep," I murmured to myself.

I shut my eyes and listened to the howling wind. Silently, I started to count backwards from one thousand. I counted slowly, picturing each number as I counted it.

Sometimes that helped clear my mind in the past.

Nine hundred ninety-seven . . . nine hundred ninety-six . . .

After a while, I drifted to sleep. But it must have been a very light sleep. The rattling sounds woke me two or three times.

I pushed my head deep into the pillow, trying to drown them out.

I slept a little more. And then I woke up — totally alert — at a different sound.

A thud. A soft scrape.

Footsteps? Moving lightly past my bed.

My breath caught in my throat. I suddenly felt cold all over.

I raised my head and listened. I pressed my

hands against the mattress and pushed myself up almost to a sitting position.

The floor creaked under someone's footsteps.

I squinted into the darkness toward the closet. Shadows moved across the floor.

I heard a click. The click of the lock on the closet door.

Shadows darkened as the door slowly slid open.

I struggled to breathe. Shudder after shudder ran down my body.

Too dark to see. No moonlight through the window.

The closet door squeaked. I heard a soft thud from inside the closet.

And then soft footsteps again. Moving toward my bed.

Someone walking very quietly. Trying to sneak past.

Shaking, I pulled myself higher. I turned to stand up.

And the dummy's face burst up in front of me. Even in the darkness, I could see the glassy eyes set on me. And the grin . . . that evil grin.

Slappy pushed his face up against mine. And rasped in a cold, harsh whisper:

"Don't mess with me, punk."

17

A weird sound escaped my throat. Like a choked *gulp*.

This couldn't be happening.

I didn't think. I just shot out my hands — and grabbed the dummy's head.

He tugged back — and I slid out of bed. As I hit the floor, the head slipped from my hands. I grabbed at the legs. My fingers wrapped around one of his little shoes.

With a loud groan, I forced myself to my feet. I was tangled in the bedcovers. My heart pounded like a bass drum.

I held my grip on the dummy's shoe. Reached out my other hand — and clicked on the bed-table lamp.

I blinked in the flash of bright light. And then I screamed:

"Brandon!"

Brandon had hold of the dummy's waist. He was trying to pull Slappy away from me.

Brandon, in his red flannel pajamas, his dark hair down over his face. His mouth twisted in a determined frown.

Brandon holding the dummy tightly, trying to sneak it out of my room.

"You —" I choked out. I swung the dummy's shoe away from me. I untangled myself from the bedsheet and moved to block Brandon's path.

"You — you —" I stammered. "What are you doing in here, Brandon? Why did you take Slappy from the closet?"

He didn't have to reply. All at once, I knew the answers. All at once — mystery solved.

I grabbed my brother's pajama sleeve. "You did *everything* — didn't you?" I said.

He took a step back. He swung the dummy onto his shoulder. Behind him, the window rattled and puffs of blowing snow slid down the glass.

I didn't let go of Brandon's sleeve. "You wrecked your own wrapping paper, right?" I said. "You trashed your own room? You put Slappy there to make it look like I did it."

Brandon kept his eyes on the floor. He didn't look at me. I saw his big shoulders heave as he let out a sigh.

"Well?" I demanded.

He didn't answer. Didn't move his eyes from the floor.

"The whole maple syrup thing," I said. "That was you, too — wasn't it!"

I squeezed his arm hard. *"Wasn't* it!" I repeated angrily.

"Okay, okay," he said finally. He pulled his arm away from me. He stuck his chin out as if challenging me. "Okay, okay. You got me."

"But — why?" I said. "Why, Brandon? I don't get it. Why did you do all this crazy stuff?"

He stared hard at me. "I just wanted to get the dummy out of the house," he said. "I wanted Mom and Dad to make you get rid of it."

"Huh?" I cried. "You're so scared of it?"

He didn't answer. "You — you just want to scare me all the time," he stammered. "That's why you bought this dummy. So I wanted Mom and Dad to make you get rid of it."

"But, Brandon —" I started.

His shoulders heaved up and down. "You made fun of me. In front of Elena," he said. "And she laughed at me."

"I'm sorry," I said. "But —"

"I wanted to pay you back," Brandon said, his voice trembling. "I wanted to get you in major trouble. So maybe next time . . ."

"You're sick," I said. "You're totally sick. Trashing your own room to get me in trouble? That's sick."

He dropped the dummy onto the edge of my bed. "Okay, okay. You're right," he said. "I was mad. I didn't think it out. I —"

"Sick," I repeated.

"Please don't tell," he said. He brushed his hair out of his eyes. "I'm sorry, Ray. I guess I was just scared. Don't tell Mom and Dad it was me — okay?"

I stared at him. My heart was still racing in my chest. I gazed at Slappy, sprawled facedown on my bed.

"Please?" Brandon begged in a tiny voice. "I'll never do anything stupid like that again. I swear."

I stared at him. I had to admit I was impressed that the big scaredy-cat had come up with such a bold plan. "Okay, okay," I muttered. "I won't tell on you."

He let out a long, shuddering sigh.

"I won't tell on you, but I'm going to do something even scarier," I said.

Brandon gasped. "Like what?"

"I'm going to bring Slappy to life *for real*!" I said.

"No, please —" Brandon grabbed my shoulder and squeezed it. "Please. Don't do it, Ray." His eyes bulged. He was really scared.

I didn't care. "Beg all you want," I said. "You did some sick, crazy things to get me in trouble. Now you have to pay."

He clasped his hands together like he was begging.

I grabbed Slappy and rolled him onto his back. His eyes gazed blankly up at the ceiling.

I pulled the sheet of paper from the jacket pocket. Unfolded it quickly. And I shouted out the strange words:

"*KARRU MARRI ODONNA LOMA MOLONU KARRANO.*"

"Now, watch," I said.

18

Nothing happened.

Brandon and I froze. Brandon's mouth hung open. I held my breath.

We both stared hard at the dummy. The strange words repeated in my ears.

I imagined Slappy twitching to life. The skinny arms and legs sliding against the bedspread. The painted grin growing wider. The glassy eyes blinking.

It would be *amazing*!

But no.

The dummy didn't move.

Of course not. Crazy things like that don't happen in real life.

Brandon's laugh broke the heavy silence. "It's just a joke!" he exclaimed.

He grabbed the paper from my hand and glanced at the words. Then he balled the paper up in his hands and tossed it to the floor.

"It's a dumb joke, Ray," he said. "And you fell for it." He picked the dummy up and shook it in my face. "You fell for it," Brandon said, shaking his head. "Who's the dummy? Who's the real dummy, Ray?"

"Go back to bed," I said angrily. "Or else I'll tell Mom and Dad what you did."

"No problem," Brandon said. He tossed the dummy at me. The wooden head clonked my forehead. The dummy fell into my lap.

"I'm not even scared of that thing anymore," Brandon said. He stomped back to his room.

I rubbed my forehead. Then I picked the paper off the floor, folded it, and stuffed it back into the dummy's jacket pocket.

I carried Slappy to the closet and shoved him behind a pile of dirty clothes. I closed the closet door behind me and crept back to bed.

The Slappy mystery was solved. I breathed a long sigh. No more problems with the dummy . . .

Wrong again, Ray. Wrong again.

"Where's my ribbon? I can't find the ribbon!" Mom shouted from the dining room.

Dad, Brandon, and I were in the kitchen. We were stuffing presents into shopping bags. "I think you used it all," Dad called to her. "Why do you need ribbon?"

"I have one more package to wrap!" Mom shouted. "Oh. Here it is. I was sitting on it."

We were already late to Elena's house. Every Christmas, there's a mad scramble to get all the presents together.

Elena's parents like to give a *ton* of presents. Mom never wants to be outdone. So we give piles of presents, too. It's a lot of fun, and they take *hours* to unwrap.

There are four of us — and five in the Shear family because Elena has twin brothers, Dustin and Justin, who are fourteen. Dad always says if we pile up all the presents, we could open a store.

Dad has a hard time with so many presents. He was very poor when he was a kid. He told us that one year for Christmas, his parents gave him a box of pretzels. His only gift. He thinks we should be happy with a box of pretzels.

Mom tells him to "get over himself."

She came into the kitchen, already in her coat. She dropped the last glittery present into a shopping bag.

"Four full bags this year," Dad said, shaking his head. "Think it's enough?"

Mom pinched his nose. "Don't be a Grinch. Let's go. We're late. We were supposed to be there at seven-thirty."

I pulled on my parka and slid the hood over my head. Brandon struggled to zip his down coat. The zipper always gets stuck.

We each carried a bulging bag outside. It had snowed for most of the afternoon, and the front yard was covered with three or four inches. A bright half moon made the snow gleam like diamonds.

The snow made nice crunchy sounds as we walked down the driveway. Elena's house is only two blocks away. No one had shoveled the walks. The street, the sidewalks, all the front yards were covered in sparkly white.

Mom and Dad always walk fast. I had to jog to keep up with them. I heard Brandon's heavy, crunching footsteps behind me.

Elena's house was brightly lit. Mr. Shear had strung pale blue lights in the tall evergreen shrubs on both sides of the front stoop. A big wreath hung in the front window.

We stamped our boots on the front stoop. I rang the doorbell. I could hear voices inside and loud music.

The door swung open. Elena poked her head out. She had a red-and-green Christmas ribbon in her hair. "Hey — you're here!" she cried. "Merry Christmas!"

We all started talking at once.

Elena stepped back to let us in. But then she

stopped. Her eyes went wide as she stared past Brandon.

"Ray, you brought your dummy!" she cried.

"Huh?" I blinked. I spun around.

Slappy sat behind me on the stoop, facing me, his lips twisted in an ugly grin.

19

"Ray — why did you bring that thing?" Mom cried.

"But I didn't —" I started.

I turned to Brandon. He had a frightened look on his face. But I knew the truth.

"*You* did it!" I cried. "*You* brought the dummy."

He shook his head. His dark hair fell over one eye. "No way!"

"I thought we were done with the dummy thing," I shouted. "Remember?" I tried to bump Brandon off the stoop with my chest. But the big hulk didn't budge.

"I didn't bring it!" he whined. "I swear!"

"What's up, guys?" Mr. Shear poked his bald head out the door. "Why is everyone on the stoop? Am I missing something?"

"The boys can't stop arguing over that stupid doll," Mom said.

"I don't know why they brought it," Dad added. "They're always fighting over it."

Then everyone started talking at once. We stepped into the house, arguing and bumping each other. I dragged Slappy in and set him on the floor next to the coat closet.

The house was warm and bright and smelled of turkey roasting in the oven. We flung our coats onto the closet floor.

Elena's brother Justin (or maybe it was Dustin) picked up Slappy. He turned to me. "I heard about this," he said. "Can you make him talk?"

"Not really," I told him.

"Then why did you bring him?"

"I didn't," I said. "Brandon did."

"Did not!" Brandon shouted.

Justin made the dummy's mouth move up and down. *"Did not!"* he made it say in a high mouse voice. He shoved the dummy into Elena's face. *"Did not! Did not!"*

Elena pushed the dummy away. "Give me a break, Justin."

"This thing is way weird," Justin said. He handed it to his brother. But Dustin wasn't interested. He set Slappy back on the floor.

Mom and Dad carried the four bulging shopping bags to the Christmas tree in front of the fireplace. Presents were already piled high around the tree.

Elena's mom burst into the room. She wore a Christmas apron over a red top and green denim jeans. "It looks like Santa's workshop around here!" she exclaimed.

Mrs. Shear always looks as if she stepped out of a tornado. Her hair is always a frizzy mess. She has a feathery voice and talks really fast like she's out of breath.

She has a pointy nose and little black eyes that are always darting around the room. She's like a fluttery bird. Elena doesn't look anything like her.

Mr. Shear has a kind, red face and a great smile. He has a big stomach that bounces in front of him when he walks fast. If he grew a white beard, he'd make a great Santa Claus.

Mom and Dad have been friends with the Shears for at least twenty years. They are like part of the family.

So the night was relaxed and fun. Lots of jokes and kidding around. A great dinner. Awesome Christmas presents.

Except for the loser GO HOOSIERS T-shirt the Shears gave me that was two sizes too big for me. Maybe it was supposed to be a joke. I don't even know what a Hoosier *is*!

Anyway, after we opened all the presents, Mrs. Shear brought out about a dozen desserts. We all sat around the living room, eating and talking quietly and listening to the crackling logs in the fire.

A great Christmas party.

And then Slappy ruined it.

20

"Ray, can you make this thing talk?" Mr. Shear held Slappy up by the arms.

"No. Not really," I murmured. I was sitting next to Elena on the couch. I could feel the warmth of the fireplace flames on my face.

"Oh, go ahead." He shoved the dummy into my lap. "Put on a show for us. That's why you brought the thing, isn't it?"

"I didn't —" I started.

"Yeah. Put on a show, Ray," Dustin said. He said it like a dare. "Be funny. Let's see you be funny."

"As funny as your face?" Slappy said.

I gasped. I didn't make him say that.

The others laughed.

"That's pretty good, Ray," Mr. Shear said. "It really looked like the dummy said that."

"How would YOU know, Fat Face?" Slappy exclaimed in his high, tinny voice. *"Your I.Q. is lower than your BELT size!"*

Mr. Shear's smile faded. "Hey, that's not funny."

"*I'll tell you what's funny, Jumbo,*" Slappy rasped. "*You trying to lift yourself out of a chair. It's like the Goodyear BLIMP going up!*"

The dummy tossed back its head and let out a long, ugly laugh.

"Ray — stop it!" Mom cried. "Why are you saying those awful things?"

"Apologize to Daniel!" Dad said.

"*I'm sorry you're such a fat, disgusting cow!*" Slappy exclaimed.

Mom and Dad both gasped. Mr. Shear's face turned purple.

Across the room, I saw Brandon studying me. He was trying to figure out what was going on.

Elena scooted away from me on the couch. "Ray," she whispered. "What are you trying to prove?"

"I didn't say those things!" I cried. "The dummy did! I swear it! The dummy did!"

I tried to toss Slappy off my lap. But his legs tangled around my arms.

The twins were the only ones laughing. Dad jumped up and started angrily across the room toward me. "Apologize," he said. "Make the dummy apologize and say something nice."

"*That was a great dinner,*" Slappy said. "*Remind me to throw up later.*"

Elena's mom shook her head. "Why are you so rude tonight, Ray?"

"*Why are you so UGLY?*" Slappy rasped.

"I didn't SAY that!" I cried. I jumped to my feet. I tried to hand Slappy to my dad. But I couldn't untangle him from my arms.

"Ray, stop," Elena pleaded. "Stop saying those horrible things."

"*It's not as horrible as your BREATH!*" Slappy screamed at her. "*You smell like something I stepped in on the way over here!*"

Elena gasped and jumped to her feet. She balled her hands into tight fists. "Why are you being so stupid?"

"*You're so stupid, you have to study up before you can BURP!*"

Mrs. Shear had her arms crossed in front of her chest. "Show is over," she said. "We get the idea, Ray."

"*Is it YOUR business, Bird Beak?*" Slappy shouted. "*Do you open cans with that nose? You're so ugly, when you were born, the doctor slapped the WRONG end!*"

"Enough! Enough!" Mom cried, tearing at her hair.

"But I'm not *doing* it!" I screamed. "You've got to believe me!"

"Give me that dummy," Dad growled. He reached out both hands for it.

I tried to hand him over. My whole body was trembling. My heart pounded in my chest.

I pushed the dummy toward my dad. And then I saw it happen like in slow motion. . . .

The dummy's heavy wooden hand swung back. As if he was moving it on his own. The hand pulled back . . .

. . . and then came flying forward.

The dummy's hand swung into my dad's forehead.

I heard a loud *CLONK* as he gave my dad a solid blow on the left temple.

Dad's eyes went wide. He let out a groan. His body folded up, and he slumped to the floor at my feet.

21

Everyone screamed and cried out and went crazy.

Mom dove to the floor beside Dad. The others huddled around them.

I tried to toss Slappy away. But he swung his fist wildly again.

I lost my balance and went stumbling across the room. The dummy tossed back his head and uttered his ugly laugh.

I heard Dad groan from down on the floor. "What happened?" he asked.

The dummy leaped from my hands. I let out a shocked gasp. Slappy was running on his flimsy legs. Running right at the Christmas tree.

"No!" I screamed. I leaped at him. He dodged away from me.

And I flew right into the tree.

The tree swayed. Ornaments clattered and clinked.

Slappy laughed as I fell into the tree. The clatter of glass became a crash.

The tree toppled onto its side beneath me.

Ornaments rolled across the carpet in all directions. Tree needles scratched my face. The strings of lights flickered out. I heard glass breaking.

I struggled to untangle myself from the prickly branches. I heard screams and cries behind me.

And when I finally tugged myself free and turned, everyone was staring in horror at me.

Dad was sitting on the carpet. Mom was hugging Brandon. The twins stood frozen, not moving a muscle. Elena had her hands to her face, her eyes shut tight.

"I — I didn't do it," I stammered. "The dummy . . ."

I glanced around the room until I spotted Slappy. He was sprawled lifelessly on his stomach, facedown on the carpet. His arms and legs were tangled beneath the trunk of his body.

"I . . . was trying to stop him," I said. "He came to life. Really. He —"

I sighed. I could see that no one believed me.

"I shouldn't have read the strange words," I said. "Brandon, tell them what I did. Tell them I'm telling the truth."

Brandon buried his face in Mom's sweater. She hugged him. I could see his shoulders trembling.

The big hulk was frightened. He wasn't going to help me.

"I guess the party is over," Mr. Shear said with a sigh. He helped pull my dad to his feet. Then they both gave me cold stares.

"I . . . don't really understand what happened here," Dad said. He rubbed his forehead. "Ray, why are you acting so crazy?"

I shook my head. "I'm trying to tell you —"

Dad took a step toward me. We heard a loud *crack*. His shoe crunched a glass tree ornament.

"Let me help you clean this mess up," Mom said.

"That's okay," Mrs. Shear said. "We'll clean up after you go."

"Yes. Please — just go," Mr. Shear said. "Deal with Ray. He has some big problems."

I turned to Elena. I saw tears running down her cheeks. She was staring at the ruined Christmas tree, broken and on its side. "Our New Year's Eve party . . ." she murmured.

"There won't be a party," Dad said. His whole face was tight. Like he was trying hard to control his anger. "I can tell you that. Ray won't be going to any parties until he can explain what came over him tonight."

Mom was still holding on to Brandon. She shook her head sadly, gazing at the mess. "Like a wild animal," she muttered. "Ray was like a wild animal."

95

I tried to get my brother's attention. But he wouldn't look at me. Brandon had to know what really happened here. But he was too frightened to say anything.

"The dummy," I murmured. "I . . . I'm really sorry. Really."

I stepped over some broken ornaments to get to Slappy. The dummy's face was buried in the carpet. He was totally lifeless. Just a doll made of wood and cloth.

I stared down at the thing, my brain spinning. I knew I wasn't totally crazy. I didn't say those horrible things that came out of Slappy's mouth. And I didn't go berserk and deliberately knock over the Christmas tree. It was totally an accident.

Should I try one more time to explain to everyone?

"The dummy came to life," I said. My voice cracked. "I didn't do any of it. The dummy —"

"Shut up, Ray!" Elena cried angrily. "Just shut up. No one is going to believe that stupid story."

She uttered a hoarse cry. "You ruined Christmas, and you ruined New Year's Eve!"

"Okay, okay," I muttered. "I give up."

I reached down and lifted Slappy off the floor. I swung the dummy over my shoulder. His wooden head hit my back.

Then, before I realized what was happening,

the head bounced back up. Slappy's grinning face slid in front of mine.

The eyes were wild. The wooden lips parted.

And he clamped his jaws tight — on my nose!

"OWWWWWWW!"

I howled in pain. The wooden mouth tightened over my nose.

I gripped the dummy by the waist and tugged. I tried to pull him away, to free myself.

But the wooden lips clamped tight, like pliers. Pain shot down my face, my neck ... my entire body.

I screamed again. "Help me! He's got my NOSE! Help me — please! It hurts! It hurts SO BAD!"

22

"Stop it, Ray," Mom shouted. "You're not funny."

"Haven't you done enough damage tonight?" Dad demanded. "Put that dummy down — now!"

"I — I can't!" I wailed.

The pain was intense. My face throbbed. My nose had gone numb.

I dropped to my knees. "H-help me . . ." I pleaded.

Blood spurted from my nose.

"He's bleeding on my white rug!" Mrs. Shear cried. "Get him off the rug!"

I felt Dad's hands grip my shoulder. He pulled me to my feet.

The dummy's mouth loosened its grip. Slappy's head slumped to one side. Lifeless again.

"Not funny, Ray," Dad whispered in my ear. "I'm very disappointed in you. Disappointed and angry." He shoved a tissue at me. I raised it to my bloody nose.

A few seconds later, we were all into our coats ... carrying shopping bags filled with our presents from Elena's family ... hurrying home in silence ... our shoes crunching on the hard, silvery snow.

The cold air made my nose sting. I kept a tissue pressed against it to stop the bleeding. The dummy bounced heavily on my shoulder as I trudged home.

"Up to your room," Mom said as soon as we arrived. "Not another word."

"We'll have a long talk in the morning," Dad said, scowling at me.

The dummy giggled.

"It's not funny!" Dad shouted. "There's nothing funny about it, Ray!"

I was too scared and too upset to tell him I wasn't the one who giggled. I didn't say a word. I ran upstairs to my room.

I shoved Slappy into the back of my closet, and I made sure the closet door was locked. Then I started to change my clothes for bed.

As I was pulling on my pajama shirt, I saw Brandon go into his room across the hall. He started to close his door, but I pushed it back open.

"Listen," I whispered, "you were right. I mean, you were right to be scared of the dummy."

His eyebrows shot up. "That was pretty weird back at the Shears' house," he said.

"We have to get the dummy out of the house," I whispered. "We have to get it as far from here as we can."

"How?" Brandon asked. "Just throw it in the trash?"

"We can't," I said. "He's alive. The dummy is alive, Brandon. He would just climb out of the trash. And he would come looking for us. Angry."

I touched my nose carefully. It was red and swollen and still throbbed with pain.

Brandon suddenly went very pale. "You really weren't pretending tonight?"

I shook my head. "I wasn't pretending. Slappy is alive, Brandon. And if we don't get him away from here, he'll ruin our lives. I know he will."

Brandon grabbed my pajama sleeve. "But, Ray — what are we going to do?"

"I — I don't know," I stammered. "I —"

Across the hall, I heard a sound that sent a shiver down my back.

Laughter. A high, shrill giggle from deep in my closet.

And then a raspy whisper: *"Slave? Come here, slave. Are you ready to obey my orders, slave?"*

23

I didn't sleep much that night. I kept listening for Slappy's voice . . . listening for the rattle of the closet door.

The next morning, I stared at the closet door and shuddered. I had to get away. I had to get out of the house to think.

How do you get rid of a living dummy who wants to make you his slave? How do you make sure he never comes back to get you?

I pulled on my parka and boots. I grabbed my snowboard from the garage. Snowboarding always clears my head.

It had snowed another couple of inches during the night. The new snow was soft and wet on top of the crunchy snow beneath. It was a cold, gray day. The sun was hidden behind heavy, low clouds.

Some of my friends like to snowboard on a steep hill at the end of our street. I was half a block away — when I heard a *THWOCK* and felt a sharp pain in my shoulder.

I spun around. Snow flew around me. It took me a few seconds to realize I'd been hit by a snowball.

Elena stood a few feet away, rubbing snow off her red wool gloves. She had on a maroon down coat that went past her knees, with the hood pulled over her head.

"You jerk!" she shouted. She scooped up snow and tossed a big handful into my face.

"Hey, give me a break —" I started.

"You jerk! You ruined everything!" she screamed. Her breath puffed up in front of her.

She heaved another handful of snow. I ducked under it.

"It wasn't my fault, Elena!" I cried.

"You ruined Christmas. And now you're ruining New Year's Eve for everyone!" she cried. "Now there's nowhere for everyone to go!"

"Maybe my mom and dad will listen to reason," I said.

"My parents think you're CRAZY!" she cried. "They think you should be locked up. Why did you say those horrible things about them?"

"I . . . didn't," I told her. "The dummy —"

She rolled her eyes. "Yeah, sure, Ray. You said the magic words, and the dummy came to life. That's not crazy or anything. That happens all the time — right?"

"Being sarcastic isn't going to help," I said.

She sighed, then she kicked a wave of snow onto my jeans. "I don't get you, Ray. Goodbye. Have a nice life." She spun around and stomped away.

"Hey, Elena — wait!"

She didn't turn back. She was swinging her arms and walking fast. Her hood flew off her head, and she didn't stop to fix it.

I watched her till she turned the corner and disappeared behind a snow-covered hedge. Then I heaved my snowboard to the ground and gave it a hard kick.

I wasn't angry at the snowboard. And I wasn't angry at Elena. If I was Elena, I wouldn't believe me, either.

I didn't feel like meeting up with my friends anymore. And I wasn't in the mood to snowboard. Seeing Elena reminded me — I had a serious problem to deal with. A *terrifying* problem right in my bedroom closet — and no one to help me.

I dragged the snowboard home and tossed it in the garage. I stamped my boots on the mat at the kitchen door and went inside.

The breakfast dishes were still on the counter. A fried egg no one wanted sat in the frying pan on the stove. "Hey, Mom? Dad?" I called.

Then I saw the note on the fridge door. It said they'd taken Brandon to a dentist appointment.

"Good," I said out loud. "Gives me time to think."

I poked my finger in the cold fried egg, then licked my finger.

I began pacing back and forth from the kitchen to the living room. Thinking hard about one question: how to get rid of a dummy for good.

When the front doorbell rang, I let out a startled cry and jumped into the air. It took a few seconds for my heart to stop pounding. Then I made my way to the front window and peered out.

A tall, thin man with curly red hair poking out from a red-and-blue Red Sox cap stood on the front stoop. He wore a plaid jacket over baggy brown cargo pants. He turned, and I saw a small coppery mustache beneath a pointy nose.

He pushed the doorbell again.

I pulled the front door open a crack and poked my head out. A gust of icy wind nearly blew the door back in my face.

"Hello? Can I help you?" I asked.

He smiled at me and adjusted his baseball cap. He gazed at me with bright green eyes.

"I think you have something that belongs to me," he said.

24

"Yes!" I cried. "Awesome!"

The green eyes squinted at me. He shoved his hands into the pockets of the plaid jacket. "Well . . . good."

"I'll get it!" I said. "Be right down."

I couldn't believe my good luck.

There I was, pacing back and forth, thinking, thinking as hard as I could. And coming up with nothing.

And then here's this stranger in a Red Sox cap at the front door, ready to rescue me from the evil dummy. What incredible timing!

With the dummy gone forever, my life would return to normal. And maybe . . . maybe if I apologized to everyone all over again, Mom and Dad would let me have the New Year's Eve party. And Elena and everyone else would be so happy.

Sweet!

I practically skipped up the stairs and across the room. I turned the lock and pulled open the closet door.

The dummy was sitting straight up with his back against the closet wall. Not where I left him. I had tossed him face-first on a pile of shirts.

He had definitely moved. It gave me a shiver of fear as I reached to pick him up.

"You're going away from here," I said. "For good."

He didn't move.

I grabbed him by the waist and pulled him up with one hand. His body slumped limply. His head bumped the floor hard as I dragged him from the closet.

I let his head bump the stairs all the way down.

Thump thump thump.

I wanted to laugh. I wanted to scream and jump up and down and do a crazy dance.

My life was about to return to normal.

I raised the dummy and held him under the armpits of his jacket. The head bobbed lifelessly on his shoulders.

I trotted to the front door and shoved Slappy at the red-haired man. "Here," I said. "Take it. And thank you."

The man's eyes went wide. He took a step back. He didn't reach for the dummy.

"That's not mine," he said.

My mouth dropped open. The dummy nearly slipped from my hands. "Excuse me?" I uttered.

"That dummy isn't mine," he repeated. He adjusted the baseball cap over his forehead. "I came to pick up Robby."

"Robby?" I squeaked.

"My dog," the man said. "Isn't this 127 Beechnut?"

"No," I said. "It's 227."

The man shrugged and gave me an embarrassed smile. "So sorry. Wrong house."

He shuffled off the stoop and hurried toward the corner.

I let out a long sigh. Slappy suddenly felt heavy in my arms. He slipped to the floor. But he didn't collapse or fold up.

He stood on his little brown leather shoes. His hands shot out stiffly at his sides. He raised his grinning face at me.

And began to laugh.

A stab of fear made my chest hurt. I gasped — and made a two-handed grab for him.

Still laughing, he dodged away. The dummy spun quickly and ran into the living room on his spindly legs.

"You can't get rid of me, slave!"

His voice was hoarse and tinny, from somewhere deep in his chest.

107

I dove at him. Grabbed for him again.

He scampered away. To the other side of the low coffee table.

"Don't try to lose me again — or you will PAY!" he screeched.

"This can't be happening!" I cried. "You can't be alive. What do you want? What do you *want*?"

"You will do as I say," he rasped, eyes darting from side to side. *"This house will be mine! If you want your family to survive, you will obey my every wish!"*

"No way!" I tried to sound angry and tough. But my voice cracked on the words. "You're going back in the closet! Then you're going far away from here."

"I don't think so," Slappy snapped.

His wooden hands wrapped around the blue fan-shaped vase on the coffee table. He raised the vase over his head.

A wave of panic tightened my throat. "Put that down!" I gasped. "That was my great-grandmother's. It's very valuable."

"Are you going to play ball with me?" Slappy cried.

"No way —" I said.

"Then I'm going to play ball with you!" he shouted. *"Catch!"*

He pulled his arm back — and heaved the vase across the room at me.

108

"Nooooo!" I let out a scream of horror. Raised both hands to catch it.

The vase bounced off my chest. Knocked my breath out. As I started to choke, it crashed onto the top of the coffee table — and shattered into a dozen jagged pieces.

"No! Oh, no!"

I heard a cry behind me.

Still struggling to breathe, I turned and saw Mom, Dad, and Brandon standing at the living room doorway. All three of them had looks of horror on their faces.

"Grandma Rose's vase!" Mom cried. She pressed her hands to her face. "I don't believe it!"

"Ray, that vase was precious!" Dad said angrily. "What *happened*?"

My whole body shook. I turned to the dummy. Slappy lay limply on his back under the coffee table.

"The dummy did it!" I screamed. "Really. The dummy did it!"

Brandon hugged himself. He kept his eyes on the floor.

Mom and Dad stared at Slappy, a lifeless wooden dummy.

Dad moved to the coffee table. He bent down and picked up a few jagged pieces of blue porcelain. He sighed and shook his head. "It can't be repaired. It's ruined."

From under the coffee table, Slappy let out a loud giggle.

"It's NOT FUNNY, Ray!" Mom shrieked. "Why are you laughing? Have you gone totally crazy? Do we have to take you to a doctor?"

Before I could answer, Slappy giggled again.

25

I spent the rest of the day in my room. Grounded. For life, probably.

Dad took the dummy and hid it away in the garage. Brandon avoided me. He stayed in his room, doing an origami project.

Elena didn't call or text me. I guessed she was still angry.

It snowed again that night. The next morning, Dad told Brandon and me to shovel the driveway. Brandon complained. He doesn't like to shovel, and he doesn't like the cold.

I kept my mouth shut. I knew I was in big trouble. No way I wanted to get in even deeper trouble.

We pulled on our parkas and boots and trudged out to the garage. The wind had blown the snow into tall drifts along the backyard fence. Snow came up to the top of my boots as we crunched our way to the garage door.

We both stopped and gazed at the door. I knew

we were both thinking the same thing: Slappy was in there. Was he waiting for us? Waiting to cause more trouble?

I shivered. Not from the cold.

"I'll open the door," Brandon said. He reached down for the handle, which was buried in snow.

"Whoa," I said. "*You* are going in there first?"

He nodded. His cheeks were red. The parka hood hid his eyes. "I made a New Year's resolution," he said. He tugged the door handle.

"What resolution?" I asked.

"You know. To be braver."

"That's awesome," I said.

He groaned as he gave the garage door handle a hard pull. Snow shifted away from the door, and it started to rise.

Another tug, and the door slid up all the way.

Brandon and I both screamed when we saw Slappy standing right in front of us. His glassy eyes seemed to glow. An evil grin spread across his wooden face.

"*Greetings, slaves!*" he shrieked. And then he raised his hands in front of him — and clicked my dad's heavy hedge clippers. "*How about a nice haircut, dudes?*"

I tried to stagger back, but my boots slid on the snow. I went down hard on my butt.

And before I could squirm away, the hedge clippers came down over my head.

SNAAAAP. SNAAAAP.

Slappy snipped the top of my parka hood off. I felt cold air on my head.

I tried to pull myself to my feet.

The hedge clippers snapped again.

"How about a nice cut?" Slappy shrieked. *"Maybe it'll teach you not to lock me in the cold!"*

I raised both hands to shield myself. The clippers came down fast. He lowered them over my face.

"NO! STOP!" I screamed. "STOP! You're going to CUT MY HEAD OFF!"

SNAAAAAP. SNAAAAAP.

26

Suddenly, the hedge clippers flew into the air. I blinked. Brandon had slapped them away. They landed with a thud in the snow and sank deep into a high drift.

"Let go of me, loser!" Slappy shrieked.

Brandon had his arms wrapped around the dummy's waist. He lifted Slappy off his feet.

"You'll pay! You'll pay for this, slave! I'm gonna chop till I drop! No more Mr. Nice Guy! Put me down!"

But Brandon shoved the dummy under his arm. Then he started to run. "Follow me, Ray. I see something!" he shouted breathlessly.

I was still plopped down in the snow. Kind of dazed, I guess, from my narrow escape. I pulled myself up, shook myself off, and started to follow Brandon.

The dummy kicked and thrashed its arms, shouting and spitting.

"You'll pay! You'll pay! I'll put your heads on snowmen! You don't know what you're doing!"

The blinding sunlight on the snow stunned my eyes. I shielded them with one glove as I trotted over the deep drifts, following Brandon.

Slappy punched the back of Brandon's parka with both fists. But Brandon held on to him tightly and kept trotting.

We reached the street, and I saw what my brother had in mind. I heard the loud roar as the big white truck came into clear view.

It was stopped in front of the Simkins' house on the corner. A big garbage truck. The truck rocked a little as its engine idled. Steam poured out of the exhaust.

Two men in gray parkas emptied trash cans into the back. A grinding roar rose up as the garbage was mashed inside.

The men dragged the empty trash cans up the long driveway.

As soon as they were gone, Brandon went into action. He carried Slappy up to the back of the truck.

"Put me down!" the dummy wailed. *"YOU'RE the garbage! Drop me! Watch out! You don't want to see me when I'm ANGRY!"*

Brandon's eyes narrowed. He gritted his jaw. Then he raised the thrashing, screaming dummy in both hands.

With a groan, he started to heave the dummy into the truck.

But Slappy twisted his body — gave a hard jerk. He slipped out of Brandon's hands and fell to the snow.

"Hey!" Brandon let out a startled cry. He grabbed for Slappy. Missed.

Slappy scrambled quickly to his feet. He swung around on his flimsy legs — and grabbed me with both wooden hands.

"Whoooooaah!" I shouted as the dummy lifted me off my feet and into the air.

How can he be so strong?

Is it his deep evil that gives him so much power?

The questions flashed through my mind. But I didn't have time to figure out the answers.

The wooden hands dug into my ribs. Before I could move or squirm or twist or cry out, the dummy raised me high over his head — and *heaved* me into the back of the grinding truck.

27

"Noooo!"

I heard Brandon's shout over the roar of the truck. He burst forward — and bumped me hard with his whole body.

I sailed over the side of the truck and landed on my back in the snow. Pain shot up my entire body.

Shaking it off, I pulled myself up — in time to see Brandon wrestling with the dummy on the ground. Grunting and groaning, they rolled over each other, making the snow fly.

"Brandon —" I called to him, struggling to my feet.

Brandon was on his back, half buried in snow. Slappy sat on top of him. The dummy raised a fist to pound my brother.

But I grabbed him around the waist. I pulled him off Brandon. And without thinking ... without really planning it, I flung the dummy with all my strength.

Slappy bounced off the back of the garbage truck. Then he slid down ... down ... and he was sucked into the truck.

Slappy kicked and screamed as he was pulled inside.

Brandon and I froze as a long, shrill howl rang in our ears. A howl of pain and horror.

And then the truck began to grind. The roar drowned out the howl.

I shut my eyes and pictured the dummy — the wood, the cloth suit jacket and pants, the little shoes — all ground up ... ground to wood shavings and bits of cloth. Mixed with the disgusting garbage.

We didn't move. We were both breathing hard. Our breath puffed up in front of us.

The grinding roar ended. Silence now.

"Hey — what are you two kids doing?"

The men were returning to their truck. One of them hoisted himself into the front cabin. The other one stared hard at Brandon and me.

"Nothing," I said. "Just watching."

He stared at us a while longer. Then he gave us a two-fingered salute and joined his partner in the truck. We watched as the truck crunched over the snow and headed up the block.

Then Brandon and I let out victory whoops and slapped knuckles and danced up and down in the snow. "Tell the truth," Brandon said. "Was I brave or was I brave?"

"You were a *superhero*!" I said.

We hurried home, dancing and laughing, tossing snow at each other. A great morning. An *awesome* morning.

"I'm never going to be scared again," Brandon said. He beat his chest with both fists and made gorilla sounds.

We both entered the house, beating our chests and grunting like gorillas. Mom and Dad thought we had gone snow crazy.

I called Elena. I apologized. I pleaded with her to come over. She appeared after lunch.

Mom and Dad greeted her and wanted to chat. But Elena and I knew we had work to do. We had to start begging — and beg better than we ever begged in our lives.

We begged and pleaded with my parents to let us have the New Year's party.

We promised to be perfect for the whole new year. We promised to help out with everything in the house — forever. We promised to make sure the basement was totally spotless after the party.

We promised everything a kid could promise. And finally, after a long, private talk with Elena's parents, Mom and Dad said yes. Go ahead and have your New Year's Eve party.

Elena and I didn't have time to celebrate our victory. We still had lots of work to do in the basement.

We hurried down there. There were still some paint cans to move out of the way. We stacked them near the walls. Then we found two brooms and swept the floor clean.

"This basement is so dark," Elena said, gazing around. "We'll need lots of colorful balloons. And some streamers across the ceiling. We have to make it look like a party."

I started to answer — but I stopped with a gasp.

From the top of the basement stairs there was rasping, evil laughter.

My heart skipped a beat. I let out a sharp cry.

We both turned to the stairs — and saw Brandon up at the top.

He tossed back his head and did his evil laugh again. He sounded just like Slappy.

"I gotcha that time," Brandon said, shaking his head. "You really thought the dummy was back." He laughed some more.

I rolled my eyes. "Brandon, just because you're brave now doesn't mean you have to scare us to death!"

That made him laugh even harder.

New Year's Eve, the basement was a whirl of colors. Elena and I put red and blue lightbulbs in all the ceiling lights. And we strung gold and silver crepe paper streamers across the low ceiling. Silver and gold helium balloons bounced against the streamers.

Music pounded. The streamers and balloons made the colored lights appear to flash and flicker. The stacks of silvery paint cans gleamed in the light and looked like party decorations.

"It looks like a nightclub — not like a basement!" Elena cried.

Kids started piling in around seven-thirty. Mom and Dad showed them the way to the basement. But my parents promised to stay upstairs.

Our friends were ready to party. We did crazy karaoke songs. We danced and hung out. We had a wild limbo contest.

Someone found a beach ball, and we had an insane volleyball game with paint cans as the net. We gobbled pizza and big bowls of chips.

Elena and I kept congratulating each other. We both agreed the party was *awesome*.

It was awesome until a little after ten o'clock.

That's when the music suddenly stopped. As if someone had pulled out the plug. And in the sudden silence, hideous, evil laughter rang out from the top of the basement stairs.

I had a mouthful of chips. The ugly laugh made me spit them all over the floor.

I spun around and shouted, "Brandon — *not* funny!"

The light was dim at the top of the stairs. I heard a step creak and saw thin legs walking down slowly, one step at a time.

"Ooh, what's that smell?" someone shouted. A sharp, putrid odor floated over the basement. Kids held their noses.

"Slappy!" I gasped.

He stopped halfway down the stairs. His gray suit was shredded. His shoes were gone. His head and shoulders were covered in scraps of garbage.

"Slappy New Year!" he screamed at the top of his lungs.

Kids gasped and cried out. A wave of fear swept over the room. My whole body shuddered.

How could he be back?

What did he plan to do?

"Th-that dummy. It's talking," someone stammered.

Everyone started talking at once. . . .

"Is it real? It's walking by itself."

"Who's making it talk?"

"Is someone inside that thing? Is it a robot?"

"Ray, is this a joke? Are you trying to trick us?"

I didn't want to answer. I knew it wasn't a joke.

Slappy lowered himself another step. Another. He took a few staggering steps across the basement floor.

The odor from the garbage made my eyes burn. Garbage scraps fell off him as he limped forward.

His evil eyes focused on me. *"You didn't invite me,"* he rasped. *"So I thought I'd CRASH!"*

He lifted a gallon can of paint off a stack. Then he swung his arm hard and sent the can sailing. It crashed against the wall, and bright yellow paint spewed out in a geyser.

"Oh, noooo," I let out a moan as the paint ran down the wall.

And before I could move, Slappy had another can open. He jerked it forward in both hands — and sent a thick wave of blue paint over three girls who were standing nearby.

They screamed as the paint swept over them. It splashed on their hair and ran down their faces.

Kids were screaming now. Backing away. Looking for hiding places.

"It's ALIVE!" a girl cried. "It's ALIVE! ALIVE! ALIVE!" She couldn't stop screaming.

Elena gasped in horror. She turned to me. "Is this really happening?"

I nodded.

Slappy staggered to a wall of paint cans. He pulled a can off the top and quickly pried the lid off.

"That's *enough*!" Elena shouted. She dove past me and tore across the room toward Slappy, both hands outstretched to stop him.

"Ohhh!" Elena screamed as she slipped in a

puddle of blue paint. Her feet slid out from under her. She went facedown in the paint.

Slappy raised a can over her and dumped a gallon of black paint on her head.

Elena gasped and choked, struggling to breathe under the thick coating of paint. I bent down beside her and tried to smear paint away from her eyes and nose.

Looking up, I saw terrified kids racing up the basement stairs.

Slappy laughed his hideous laugh and heaved another tidal wave of paint over two boys trying to hide under the food table.

"We have to get out of here!" a boy shouted.

"It's ALIVE! It's ALIVE!" the girl continued to scream.

Slipping and sliding in the thick paint, kids stampeded up the stairs.

I saw a boy reach the top. He grabbed the doorknob. I saw him struggling. Pushing. Pulling.

Two other kids jammed beside him. I saw them start to pound on the door.

"It's *locked*!" someone screamed. "The door — we can't open it! Help! We're locked in!"

29

A wave of black paint sailed at my head. I ducked, and it splashed onto my back.

Kids screamed and cried and pounded the basement door.

Where were my parents? They had mentioned going next door for a few minutes to say Happy New Year to the Willards. . . .

Slappy tossed back his head in a hyena laugh and sent another gallon of paint splashing over the kids on the stairs. The paint covered their heads and made them splutter and choke.

"Treat me like GARBAGE?" Slappy shrieked. *"You'll all end up in the garbage!"*

Brandon — brave now — dove forward to tackle the cackling dummy. But he slid on the paint-drenched floor. Fell and cracked his head on the hard concrete.

"Brandon?" I screamed.

I heard a loud banging and then excited cries. I raised my eyes to the top of the stairs and saw the basement door fly open. Elena, covered in black paint, began to lead kids out the door.

Slappy heaved a gallon can of paint up the stairs at them. Kids shrieked and ducked. A girl went toppling headfirst down the sticky, wet steps. That made the dummy laugh even harder.

I dropped down beside Brandon. "Are you okay?"

He raised his head groggily. "I guess so." He had purple and green paint in his hair and down one side of his face.

I helped him to his feet. He rubbed a hand back through his paint-soaked hair.

Kids were frantically trying to get to the basement stairs. Slappy had three boys trapped against the food table. He was menacing them with a can of white paint.

Suddenly, I had an idea. Slappy had his back turned to Brandon and me. It was easy to slip behind him.

I pulled my brother behind a wall of paint cans. "Push!" I said. "We'll push together."

Brandon squinted at me. "Huh?"

"If we can push this wall of cans on Slappy, maybe we can crush him under them."

Brandon shook his head. "But the garbage truck didn't crush him."

"Maybe we can at least *stop* him," I said. "Come on. It's worth a try."

The heavy cans were stacked about a foot over

my head. Brandon and I leaned our shoulders against the wall of cans.

"On the count of three," I said. We both took deep breaths. "One . . . two . . . THREE!"

We lunged forward. Heaved our shoulders against the cans.

And . . . yes! The whole wall toppled over.

Slappy let out a high, shrill wail as the wall caved in on him. Burying him . . . crushing him under its weight.

I watched him crumble to the floor. The paint cans thudded on top of him. He disappeared beneath them.

Silence now.

Brandon and I stood together, staring at the pile of paint cans.

Did we really defeat him?

30

I gazed around. No one else in the basement.
Everyone else had escaped. Brandon and I were
the only ones still here.

I shuddered. We were both drenched in thick
paint.

I rolled a can of paint out of my way with one
shoe. Then I bent down to examine the cans on
the floor.

And a wooden hand shot up from under the
cans and grabbed me by the throat.

"*Aaaaach!*" I uttered a choked scream as the
hand tightened its grip.

Slappy sat up. His evil, red-lipped grin
appeared to spread over his face.

"Ch-choking me . . ." I gasped.

The hand tightened. My neck throbbed. I
struggled to suck in air. "Choking . . ."

The dummy grinned up at me. I tugged hard.
Pulled back with all my might.

But Slappy had evil strength. I couldn't free myself from the hard wooden hand.

"Where are you going? The party is just starting!" the dummy declared.

"Ch-choking . . ." I gasped.

"Slappy New Year! Slappy New Year to both of my slaves!"

I knew I was passing out. I saw bright yellow. And then the room started to fade away.

Brandon grabbed my waist and tried to pull me free. But Slappy was too strong.

I thrashed my arms wildly. I tried to punch the dummy. My hand slid to his jacket pocket.

The room was spinning darkly now. I actually saw bright yellow stars before my eyes.

My hand tore at the dummy's jacket pocket. And without realizing it, I pulled out the folded sheet of paper.

The paper with the strange words on it. The words that brought the evil dummy to life.

If we read the words again, will they put him back to sleep?

Frantically, I pushed the paper at my brother. "Read . . ." I choked out. "Read . . ."

Did Brandon understand me?

Yes.

He grabbed the paper from my hand. His fingers struggled to unfold it.

The room spun. The bright stars swam in front of me. Darkness . . . darkness . . .

I saw Brandon raise the paper to his face. His eyes went wide.

"Read . . ." I choked out.

He squeezed my arm. "Ray," he said, "I can't read the words. They're covered in paint!"

31

Slappy tossed his head back and laughed. *"Losers!"*

He let go of my throat and made a grab for the paper.

It flew out of Brandon's hands and fluttered to the floor.

Slappy and I both dove for it. I grabbed it first. I swung it away from Slappy. Held it above my head. Light from the ceiling poured through the paper.

And I realized I could see the words through the paint!

"'KARRU MARRI ODONNA LOMA MOLONU KARRANO!'"

My voice was hoarse, but I shouted them as loud as I could.

Slappy made a sound like air going out of a balloon. His head tilted back. His legs collapsed. He sank to the floor. His head hit hard and bounced a couple of times.

Then he didn't move.

I rubbed my sore neck. I took a deep breath and tried to stop my heart from thudding in my chest. Brandon stood silently beside me, staring down at the lifeless dummy.

"We did it," I said. "We defeated him."

"Happy New Year," Brandon whispered.

We didn't have time to celebrate.

I heard a sound — and saw Mom and Dad at the top of the stairs. Even in the dim light, I could see the look of horror on their faces.

"This . . . this can't be!" Mom cried, gazing at the paint-splotched room. The walls were all splashed. The floor had lakes of paint everywhere.

She slipped on paint and started to fall down the stairs. She bumped into Dad. They both grabbed the banister to keep their balance.

"Oh, no . . . Oh, no . . . Oh, no . . ." Mom moaned. "What did you do down here? Ray, how did this *happen*?"

"We're ruined," Brandon whispered. "We're dead meat."

They made their way onto the basement floor. They walked slowly, careful not to step in paint. But it was impossible. The whole floor was covered.

"Where are the other kids?" Dad demanded. "How did this happen?"

I glanced at the dummy, sprawled on the floor.

"The party just got out of control," I murmured. "I'll clean it all up, Dad. I promise. I'll stay down here till the basement is perfect again."

"All this paint," Mom muttered, shaking her head. "All this paint everywhere. It's impossible. It can't be!"

Mom and Dad gazed around the basement, muttering to themselves and shaking their heads. Finally, Dad said, "We can clean it up."

"I guess . . ." Mom murmured.

"Let's give the kids a break," Dad said. "It's New Year's."

"Yes! Happy New Year!" I cried. *Were we actually getting away with this?*

"Happy New Year!" Brandon joined in.

We all cheered.

And actually, there was a lot to cheer about. The evil dummy had been put to sleep. And . . . we had thrown a New Year's Eve party no one would ever forget!

The next morning, Brandon, Dad, and I cleaned up the basement the best we could. Dad said once the paint dried, it would make a great party room. He said he just liked seeing so many colors at once.

Dad has always been weird — thank goodness!

Brandon and I still couldn't get the paint off

our hands or faces or hair. Dad said that might take a while.

That afternoon, I pulled on my parka and boots and started for the garage. Mom stopped me in the kitchen. "Where are you going, Ray?"

"Snowboarding," I said. "I'm meeting Elena and some other kids."

"I put that dummy back in your room," Mom said. "I put it in your closet."

"But I told you I don't want it anymore," I replied.

"Okay," Mom said. "Should we keep it in a trunk in the basement in case you change your mind?"

"No. No way!" I said. "Get rid of it. Please — give it away or something. I really don't want it."

"I found a sheet of paper with the dummy," Mom said. "It had the strangest words on it. Very hard to pronounce."

Pronounce?

I gasped in horror. My whole body went cold.

"Mom!" I cried. "You didn't read those words out loud — did you? Mom? Did you? Did you? Did you read the words out loud?"

EPILOGUE

EPILOGUE

I tore off my parka, tossed it on the floor, and ran up to my room. I expected to see Slappy standing in the doorway, ready to pounce at my throat.

I stopped at the landing and listened. Silence.

I crept to my room. No. He wasn't standing there. My skin tingled with fright. Where was he hiding?

I gazed all around the room. Everything was just as I'd left it. My paint-stained clothes from the party were still in a heap on the floor.

I crossed to the closet. Mom said she'd put Slappy in there.

I gripped the closet doorknob. Should I open it?

A chill ran down my back. I took a deep breath and swung the door open all the way.

I squinted into the dark closet. My eyes glanced over the piles of T-shirts and sweaters and jeans on the shelves.

I pulled the light cord and the light flashed on. I lowered my eyes to the floor.

No. No sign of him.

I stepped into the closet, pushing jackets out of the way. I made my way to the back. I gazed all around.

Gone. Slappy was gone.

Not where Mom put him. Not in my room.

I backed out of the closet. "Slappy?" I called. "Are you here? Are you still here?"

Silence.

Gone.

But what was that green-yellow glow on my bookshelf?

I stumbled over the paint-stained clothes as I made my way across the room.

The Horror. The little Horror that old man at HorrorLand had given me . . . It was glowing brightly, as if on fire.

A shiver of fear shook my body. I couldn't take my eyes off the light.

The green-yellow light — so strange, so cold — pulled me. I could feel myself pulled into the light. It spread all around me until all I could see was its eerie glow.

And then it faded away, faded like a dying campfire. And I was standing somewhere else. Not standing in my room.

Blinking hard, shivering, I gazed around. And

recognized the shelves of strange objects and souvenirs.

Chiller House. I was standing in that little shop, back in HorrorLand.

And the old man, the shop owner, Jonathan Chiller stood over me, a broad smile on his pale face.

"Welcome back, Ray," he said in his high, croaky voice. "You're right on time. The game is about to begin."

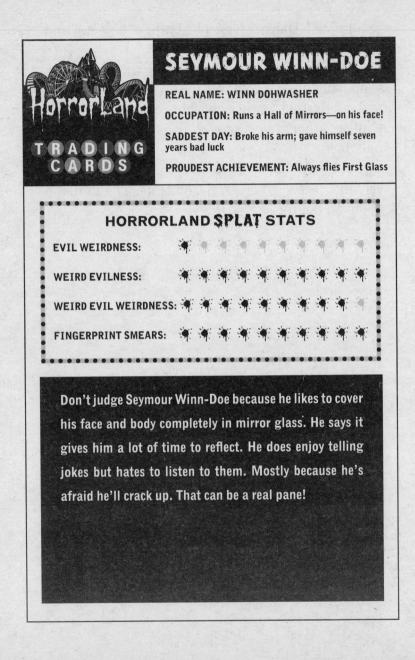

SEYMOUR WINN-DOE

REAL NAME: WINN DOHWASHER

OCCUPATION: Runs a Hall of Mirrors—on his face!

SADDEST DAY: Broke his arm; gave himself seven years bad luck

PROUDEST ACHIEVEMENT: Always flies First Glass

HORRORLAND SPLAT STATS

EVIL WEIRDNESS:

WEIRD EVILNESS:

WEIRD EVIL WEIRDNESS:

FINGERPRINT SMEARS:

Don't judge Seymour Winn-Doe because he likes to cover his face and body completely in mirror glass. He says it gives him a lot of time to reflect. He does enjoy telling jokes but hates to listen to them. Mostly because he's afraid he'll crack up. That can be a real pane!

Ready for More?

Well, well . . . Ray isn't alone, you know. Six kids have fallen into Jonathan Chiller's trap. Why has he brought them back to HorrorLand?

To play a game — the most terrifying game of their lives. Maybe they should have paid for their souvenirs on their first visit to his shop. Because now Chiller says it's "payback" time. If Ray and the others don't win his game, they may pay with their lives!

Don't miss the most frightening HorrorLand adventure yet — Goosebumps HorrorLand #19: *The Horror at Chiller House.*

About the Author

R.L. Stine's books are read all over the world. So far, his books have sold more than 300 million copies, making him one of the most popular children's authors in history. Besides Goosebumps, R.L. Stine has written the teen series Fear Street and the funny series Rotten School, as well as the Mostly Ghostly series, The Nightmare Room series, and the two-book thriller *Dangerous Girls*. R.L. Stine lives in New York with his wife, Jane, and Minnie, his King Charles spaniel. You can learn more about him at www.RLStine.com.

THERE'S ALWAYS ROOM FOR ONE MORE SCREAM!

An all-new series from fright-master R.L. Stine!

SCHOLASTIC

SCHOLASTIC and associated logos
are trademarks and/or registered
trademarks of Scholastic Inc.

www.scholastic.com/goosebumps

GBHOH6

NOW A MAJOR
MOTION PICTURE

JACK BLACK

Goosebumps

VILLAGE ROADSHOW PICTURES

THIS FILM IS NOT YET RATED. FOR FUTURE INFO GO TO FILMRATINGS.COM

f /GoosebumpsTheMovie

SCHOLASTIC

COLUMBIA PICTURES

SCHOLASTIC and associated logos
are trademarks and/or registered
trademarks of Scholastic Inc.

www.EnterHorrorLand.com

GBHL19B

THE SCARIEST PLACE ON EARTH!

SCHOLASTIC and associated logos
are trademarks and/or registered
trademarks of Scholastic Inc.

SCHOLASTIC
www.EnterHorrorLand.com

GBHL19B

Catch the
MOST WANTED
Goosebumps® villains
UNDEAD OR ALIVE!

SCHOLASTIC, GOOSEBUMPS and associated logos are trademarks and/or registered trademarks of Scholastic Inc. All rights reserved.

■SCHOLASTIC
scholastic.com/goosebumps

Available in print
and eBook editions

GBMW9